Blood for Blood

THOMAS WAUGH

© Thomas Waugh 2021.

Thomas Waugh has asserted his rights under the Copyright, Design and Patents Act, 1988, to be identified as the author of this work.

First published in 2021 by Sharpe Books.

CONTENTS

Chapters 1 – 21
Epilogue

BLOOD FOR BLOOD

"Sooner or later, one has to take sides. If one is to remain human."
Graham Greene, *The Quiet American.*

1.

Summer.

The light was fading – being snuffed out like candles, after evensong. The swollen sky resembled a fresh bruise. Rain spat against the window, like the sound of a thousand rifle stocks clacking against the ground during a drill.

James Marshal was perched upon a stool in *The Tap-In* – a sports bar in South-East London. The décor was modern, but the locals created an atmosphere similar to an old-fashioned pub. Their resident chef, Olly, also cooked up the best Cuban sandwiches south, or north, of the river. The establishment stocked a healthy range of German beers on draught. More than one - or rather more than a half-dozen - of Marshal's former girlfriends had claimed that he drank too much. Marshal liked to think that he drank just the right amount. Or not quite enough. The ex-Paratrooper ordered a brandy and pint of beer. He yawned, again. He had stepped out for the evening to help wash away boredom, rather than drown any sorrows. Or he was afflicted by a bone-deep melancholy, nagging him in the background like a fishwife. If his soul were a musical instrument, it would have been a pedal steel guitar. Marshal could have denied he had a soul, if he did not occasionally hear the mournful sound it made. His heart sometimes felt as heavy as the thick-bottomed tumbler the barman, Ross, had poured his brandy into. Marshal was not sure when he had last felt alive. Or he did. It was when he had last killed someone.

The ex-soldier, who had served in 3 Para, had killed over a dozen members of the Taliban in Helmand. Marshal wasn't necessarily proud of the number of confirmed kills he had racked up in Afghanistan. But he did not feel shame, or guilt, either. He preferred they were dead, to his brothers-in-arms or any innocent Afghanis. People were forever bleating about how awful and "wicked" Donald Trump and Boris Johnson were. They could do with being introduced to the Taliban, for context, Marshal judged. Marshal had seen the aftermath of the Taliban having eviscerated mothers for sending their daughters to school – and homosexuals castrated with butchers' knives. One village elder was beaten to death too, for retrieving water from a well to give to a dehydrated American soldier.

Marshal never hesitated and never missed.

"Do you enjoy killing the enemy?" an owlish counsellor, who had to keep pushing his glasses up the bridge of his nose from the sweat running down his face, posed during a designated therapy session at Camp Bastion.

"I enjoy not being shot by the enemy," the soldier replied, before yawning out of boredom or contempt.

Marshal's last kill had not occurred in Helmand, however. It had been on the streets of South London. He had gunned down three members of the Albanian mafia, after they had threatened to execute him and his girlfriend, Grace. Marshal did not hesitate or miss, as he emptied his Glock 21 into the murderous trio. He had started and ended the war against the criminal gang, after an Albanian drug dealer had dared to flick a cigarette butt at Marshal. The spark ignited a fire inside the soldier.

"Well, I get up in the morning and I get my brief
I go out and stare at the world in complete disbelief
It's not righteous indignation that makes me complain
It's the fact that I always have to explain..."

Thankfully, Van Morrison drowned out the din of the football fans at the far end of the bar - crowing or offering up feigned despair over a throw-in.

Marshal took another swig of his brandy, not knowing if the alcohol was quelling or fuelling the dull ache in his stomach. It was the same dull ache he felt during the last months of his career in the army. Perhaps it was the equivalent of a five-year itch. Something was calling him to action. Marshal sometimes felt like he was a gun, laying too dormant – waiting to be fired.

"You will not go far in the army with your current attitude," his commanding officer asserted, after giving him a well-rehearsed but uninspiring lecture in relation to following orders. Marshal (just about) respected the man, who religiously collected biographies of the Duke of Marlborough – and had famously, or infamously, carried out an affair with his sister-in-law.

"I hope that's a promise rather than a threat," Marshal drily replied, having already decided that his current tour would be his last. Choosing to enlist in the army had been one of the best decisions he had ever made. But leaving the army had been another.

One of the other locals, Paul, walked in the bar and sat next to Marshal. It was difficult to tell which thing Paul loved the most - beer or Chelsea FC. It depended on their league position and how much he had drunk during any given evening. He was a good man, who could stand a round - and make and take a joke. The two friends greeted each other, and Marshal gave Ross a nod to get a round in, including one for the barman. Ross was on the cusp of celebrating or commiserating. His claim to fame was that he had been one of the first actors to play Simba in the London stage production of *The Lion King*. Ross had recently auditioned for the part of Mufasa and was waiting on news of a call back. "It's the circle of life," he had half-joked.

"How's Grace?" Paul asked, asking after Marshal's girlfriend, who occasionally came down to the *Tap* for a drink. The former model was a welcome sight – and could make and take a joke herself. No matter how gripping the match, few customers remained glued the screen when she walked into the bar. Men leered. Women sneered.

"She has been away, in New York, visiting friends. Grace has the wisdom to spend some time away from me. You can have too much of a good - or mediocre - thing. She's back tomorrow, though. I'm cooking her a meal. If the sight of me doesn't turn her stomach, then my chilli con carne might," Marshal remarked, the joke or the thought of Grace bringing a smile to his face. The forty-plus year old suddenly appeared five years younger.

"She's a great gal, one in a million. Far too good for you, of course. Are you thinking of making an honest woman of her, though?"

Initially, cynically, Marshal thought that "honest woman" might be an oxymoron. The smile briefly fell from his expression, like ice cream running down a child's hand during a sweltering afternoon, as the prospect of marriage loomed large in his brain, like a tumour. The dull ache in his stomach increased. "The marriage hearse," William Blake wrote. Now there was an oxymoron. Marshal was in little doubt that he loved Grace. He did not want anyone else. But everlasting love was another likely oxymoron. Marshal was all too aware of his inability to remain faithful to a cause or person – for five weeks, let alone five years or more. He had abandoned his education and various intellectual pursuits – despite having attended Harrow, Magdalen, and Sandhurst. He cut short his career in the army. He must have written the first three chapters to at least half a dozen novels. But no fourth chapter. After the army Marshal worked as a PMC (Personal Military Contractor) in

Iraq and Afghanistan, as well as doing a stint for the shipping companies hunting down Somali pirates. But nothing was long-term, permanent - or purposeful. Like his relationships. When he returned to England, Marshal was hired by the fixer, Oliver Porter. Porter arranged for the former soldier to serve as a close personal protection officer. But, again, his heart was not in it. He was as constant as Cressida – or Charlie Sheen. Loving Grace today was no guarantee of loving her tomorrow. And what if they brought a child into the world? Did Marshal want to bring a child into the world? A world in which Jeremy Corbyn and Grant Shapps existed. He would not be able to keep both a gun and child in the house at the same time. He even employed some warped reasoning and flirted with the idea that it was better to break things off – to hurt Grace a little now instead of hurting her a lot in the future. Marshal could count the number of successful marriages he knew of on one hand. Divorce rates were as high as his cholesterol levels. Grace would know just as few successful long-term relationships, but still he sensed that she would prefer to be married. No one wanted to live in sin, albeit everybody did in some way, he darkly mused. Was there not a part of him which wanted to be married too, to sanctify their bond in a house of God? Catholicism ran through Marshal, like veins through a block of marble.

"If she can make an honest man out of me in return, then Grace will be one in a trillion," Marshal countered, regaining his humour and composure.

2.

The rain abated. The starless sky was now mottled, like an antique gun barrel. Marshal downed another brandy and left the bar. He had a lunch with an old friend, Jack "Nails" Foster, the next day. There were several rumours pertaining to his nickname. Some explained that he was as hard as nails. Others that he once killed an assailant with a nail gun. Others that he had disarmed a nail bomb in a pub in Belfast. Foster neither confirmed nor denied any of the stories. It was unlikely to be a dry lunch. The idea of a dry lunch was anathema, or an oxymoron, to the former member of the SAS, Marshal thought. There had been an edge to Foster's voice when Marshal had spoken to him over the phone. The soldiers would drink, until the edge was tempered.

Marshal walked home; head bowed down like a mourner. The temperature had dropped, but not so dramatically that his shoulder, injured from a bullet received in Helmand, began to stiffen. His square jaw was dusted with stubble and his light brown hair (cut short, but not army short) was peppered with a few, or more than a few, grey hairs. His brown eyes appeared tired or, at best, wistful. His expression may have often been world weary, but thankfully Marshal could still laugh along with the joke of life. It was important to laugh in the face of a pernicious world, otherwise you became the punchline. Beneath a dark blue sports jacket, with a dog-eared copy of Graham Greene's *Gun for Sale* poking out of the pocket, Marshal wore a black polo shirt which Grace had bought for him. She knew what he liked. He also wore some faded jeans which, like their owner, had seen better days. What with it being South London, he also wore a pair of white Reeboks.

Marshal had lit a cigarette, within a few steps after leaving *The Tap-In*. He smoked less since meeting Grace but couldn't quite wholly quit. He liked to smoke after eating, after sex, and in between drinks. The cigarette often ousted any bitter taste in his mouth, from tedium or misanthropy. When Oliver Porter once asked, "You don't particularly like people, do you James?" Marshal wryly replied: "I can't believe that anyone can much like people, after getting to know them. Life is a sexually transmitted disease."

Neon flickered in the takeaway signs. Grim, jowly faces peered out of grimy bus windows. Pasty youths glared, mesmerised, into phone screens, barely avoiding being run over by Prius after Prius gliding by, waiting for the latest Uber customer to book a ten-minute journey. London churned out more vacuity and selfishness than petrol fumes. Clusters of cranes, like groups of steel, skeletal dinosaurs, loomed large on the horizon - building and destroying the capital at the same time. The circle of life. Gigantic glass and aluminium phalluses also littered the landscape, appearing like a computer-generated backdrop to an underwhelming, utopian sci-fi film. But modernity was a veneer, the caked-on make-up of a drab. It is always difficult to polish a turd. Antifa had not quite created paradise yet. London was still a mix of Vanity Fair and the Slough of Despond, Marshal considered - all the worse for so few of its inhabitants being familiar with John Bunyan and *The Pilgrim's Progress*.

Marshal's phone vibrated. He grinned. It was a message from Grace.

Just arrived at another dinner party. Hiding in the toilet. Trump has just been compared to Hitler and someone has boasted that she uses the same eyeliner as one of the Kardashians. I miss you. Don't drink too much tonight. On second thoughts, do drink too much. It'll make it easier for me to take advantage of you. xx

He replied:

I miss you too. Am picturing you wearing an "I like Ike" campaign badge and a short skirt that's tighter than a Scotsman. xx

Grace replied:

You are awful. But I like you. xx

Marshal put his phone back in his pocket and crossed the road, deciding to take a shortcut back to his flat. He headed into a backstreet, which would have been ill-lit even if it did not run beneath a railway arch. Pigeon shit covered the pavement like a bad, or highly regarded, Jackson Pollock painting. The air reeked of piss, weed and pizza. The alleyway was deserted, or rather almost deserted.

Even after a few drinks the ex-soldier was more aware of his surroundings than most. It was his training, partly. As much as weariness sometimes infused his bones, wariness had been grafted onto him, like a tree developing a new branch. His eyes had learned to flit left and right each time he entered a village or crossed a road in Helmand. During his time as a close protection officer Marshal was accustomed to assessing the entrances and exits to each location and taking in any suspicious, or innocent looking, figures inhabiting the space.

The first figure occupying the alleyway sat upon a moped, tapping away on his phone but occasionally, furtively, glancing up. The youth wore an open-faced helmet. Gaunt. Foreign. Dressed in a Man Utd top, beneath a stained leather jacket. His teeth were yellow, as if he swished urine around in his mouth every morning. Greasy, black curls poked out of the helmet.

Another figure, well-built but ill-dressed in a purple puffer jacket and grey tracksuit bottoms, stood on the other side of the street. They looked like brothers, or cousins, Marshal considered. He noted a skull tattoo on his thick neck. His nose was as crooked as a hedge fund. He buried his hands in his pockets. Perhaps he was trying to keep them warm, perhaps he was clasping a knife. His head was shaved, his features as hard as gnarled bones. He looked unpleasant. He was unpleasant.

Marshal remembered Ross mentioning how the area had suffered a recent spate of mobile phone and laptop thefts. One man would snatch an item and then quickly jump on the back of his confederate's motorbike. Or the two of them would ride past their victims and grab the phone or laptop from a table. Some locals, mainly women, had also been robbed at knifepoint. *The Southwark News* had covered the latest crime spree, reporting that the police believed the suspects to be Romanian – although no arrests had been made.

Toma had sat on his moped and witnessed the man put his phone in his pocket, cross the street and head towards the alley. It would be easy pickings. He sent his cousin, Luca, a text message – reminding him to take his wallet and watch, as well as phone. Once the mugging was finished, they would ride over to Camberwell – and then Dulwich and Peckham Rye. They had already pinched devices from Blackfriars and Waterloo earlier in the evening. Their aim was to steal a dozen items by the end of the night. If they somehow got caught the authorities would try – but fail – to deport them. Most victims probably did not even bother to report the thefts to the police. Their insurance would cover things. They would get a new phone, or an upgrade.

"We are doing them a favour," Toma half-jested to his cousin, a month ago, when they had started the enterprise.

The pair were not affiliated with any gang, but Toma's goal was to join the Romanian mafia. He dreamed of being a pimp – and unconsciously licked his lips every time he imagined the scenario. He would have sex with the girls whenever he wanted and earn more money than he ever could if he had remained in his village, just outside of Brasov. Toma envisioned himself working his way up in the organisation. The benefits system was generous - too generous - in England. The trained carpenter had originally come to London to find work and send money back to his family. But crime paid better. His favourite film was *Scarface*, having watched it over ten times in the past year.

Luca enjoyed the look of fear in his victim's eyes as he snatched their phone or purse – and the blade of his knife loomed large in their terrified expressions. The stuck-up English women, who usually looked down their noses at the Romanian, appeared as frightened as little girls. He relished the power. The usually stern-faced thug would break out into a grin when his victims would scream or sob, as he climbed on the back of the bike and sped away. They would have good/profitable night again, Luca judged. He thought of some of his friends, who had travelled over from Romania, who worked as kitchen porters or cab drivers. They toiled endless hours for little reward. They were fools, as weak as women. Luca would go out tomorrow evening and enjoy the fruits of his labour. Beer. Cocaine. He would book a prostitute again. London was the promised land.

Marshal passed the point of no return. There had been a moment when he had registered the prospective danger – and he could have turned back onto the main road and relative safety. Some say that once a Catholic, always a Catholic. And once a Para, always a Para. The regiment's motto was "Ready for Anything". When the regiment was founded in 1942, Churchill described the soldiers as "men apart". They were the first to fight and the last to leave the battlefield. Marshal was never going to turn back and re-join the main road. No retreat. No surrender. Part of him wanted the suspect figures to attack him – so he could attack them in return. Hurt them. Take them out of action, like the Taliban. He wanted to deliver justice – and feel alive. He never went looking for trouble, Marshal told himself, but he was content for trouble to find him.

Marshal's square jaw became squarer, as he clenched his teeth. His hand balled into a fist, knuckles cracking. The words of various instructors, from his time in the army, milling, chimed in his ears. *Controlled aggression.*

Toma nodded to Luca to set off after their quarry. The brutal thug intended to grab the Londoner's coat, twist him around and punch him in the face, without a word said. His victim would hand over everything, whilst still in shock. If the Englishman hesitated, Luca would pull the knife from his pocket. If he tried to fight back, then the Romanian would use the knife. He had stabbed opponents before. It was stab, or be stabbed, back on the streets of Brasov, when opposing gangs or football fans clashed. He had scarred people for life, without a moment's regret. If his initial blow knocked the Englishman out, then the burly Romanian would duly search through his pockets for his phone and wallet. He would check for a watch worth selling on too, to a pawnbroker they regularly dealt with - who was more than comfortable with selling stolen goods.

Toma sniffed - trying to mine any remnants of cocaine from his nostrils - and got ready to start the bike. The revving of the engine would drown out any noise emanating from underneath the railway arch.

Luca wore black trainers. His footsteps were quick but quiet on the pavement as he moved up behind the Englishman. But not quite quiet enough. Marshal turned around as his assailant was half a dozen paces away. Usually, his victims flinched or cowed when the imposing, intimidating figure of Luca approached his prey. Or they tried to run away. But the

Englishman advanced towards the Romanian, covering the ground between them in the blink of an eye.

Instead of using his fist to strike his opponent, for fear of breaking his hand, Marshal swung his elbow around into the Romanian's face, breaking his nose. Cartilage split through skin. Luca remained on his feet, his neck acting like a shock absorber. Before his opponent could recover from the initial blow, the Englishman buried his foot into his groin – and then followed-up with a few punches. Marshal resisted hitting Luca as hard as he could. But he hit him hard enough. The Romanian staggered and fell. The back of his head struck the asphalt with a sickening crack, further disorientating and weakening him. Marshal needed to put the man down - methodically and viciously - before his confederate entered the fray. Which he did.

Toma's face was twisted in malignancy and fury, as if his features had been turned in a kaleidoscope. The Romanian spat out a curse as he witnessed events unfold. Unravel. A couple of victims had tried to run or futilely attack Luca before. But this was different. Dire. Toma dismounted from the bike and raced over, to defend his cousin and attack the Englishman.

The Romanian spat out another curse in his native language and drew a kitchen knife. Marshal saw the blade. It would be fight rather than flight. His mind and body became even more alert, his brain awash with endorphins. Before his new opponent reached him, he took off his jacket and held it up, like a matador would his cape, away from his body.

"Drop the knife, or I will use it on you," Marshal warned, his voice remarkably calm – making a promise rather than a threat.

A flicker of doubt entered Toma's aspect. There may have been a moment when he thought that he and Luca could withdraw. But he had passed the point of no return.

Toma thrust the kitchen knife forward, half distracted by the coat. Marshal moved to the side but then sprang forward, quickly wrapping his jacket around the assailant's weapon and tattooed hand. Marshal then butted his opponent on the chin, making sure not to connect with the crash helmet. The knife and coat fell to the ground, as did Toma after a knee struck him in the groin. The Romanian's face was now contorted in agony, as if he were attempting to win a gurning competition.

Toma groaned, like a drunk laid out in the gutter. Marshal, as impassive as a stoic, picked up the knife and coat. He placed his knee on the mugger's chest, pinning him down, and stuffed a sleeve of his jacket into his mouth.

"If you struggle or scream, I am going to slit your throat. Understand?" Marshal remarked, with more than a hint of menace, placing the edge of the blade against Toma's neck, slick with perspiration. Marshal proceeded to cut, or carve, off the Romanian's index finger. The same finger which had tapped out the order for Luca to rob the Englishman. Toma's eyes widened and watered, with more than a hint of pain and terror. Blood gushed and then oozed. The gory digit appeared forlorn and lonely on the road, like a corpse abandoned on a battlefield.

"If I see you in the area again, I will cut off your hand. Understand?"

Marshal could not be sure if his victim was nodding his head, or writhing in torment.

"Put pressure on the wound and elevate," he added. Toma could not be sure if his assailant was being sincere in his advice - or mocking him. It might have been both.

Luca stirred. Marshal removed Toma's crash helmet, walked over and brutally smashed it into the thug's face, without pause or ceremony – like a man going about his business. He broke his nose, again – splitting open the gash even more. Luca blacked out. As much as adrenaline coursed through his body –

more toxic or addictive than nicotine or alcohol – Marshal kept a level head. A twinge of regret flickered in his expression, however, when he noticed how blood had spurted upon the paperback, which still hung out of his jacket pocket. Marshal collected up the coat, knife, and the Romanians' wallets. He noticed a curtain twitch in a second-floor window, but it could have just been the wind.

Marshal took his leave, to the sound of Toma either mumbling curses or whimpering. Luca lay on the road like a large piece of refuse, waiting to be scraped-up and taken away. A train rumbled overhead, like rolling thunder, as the heavens opened.

Rain splattered against Marshal's face, but he barely noticed – his expression as unmoved as a stone effigy, a death mask. Thankfully, the heavy rain washed the blood from his hands. There was also a small cut on his knuckle, from where his fist had connected with his opponent's teeth. Once he disposed of the coat, knife and, irritatingly, the stained paperback, Marshal thought of Grace and permitted himself an almost imperceptible smile.

How was your night? xx Grace texted, as he reached his apartment building on Amelia St.

Marshal replied:

Uneventful. Xx

3.

Marshal slept fitfully. The encounter with the Romanians still prickled in his thoughts, like static. He could not say whether he had enjoyed punishing his attackers, but he was satisfied. The only regret Marshal experienced was that he had not tortured or frightened the thugs enough, considering how much suffering they had heaped upon others. Weighing their crimes against their punishment, had he not been too merciful? Or Marshal failed to sleep because of the infernal heat, as irritating and stinging as a swarm of bees. A fan helped. But not enough. He still craved the warmth of the figure who often slept on the other side of the bed. A couple of nights ago he found himself spraying the bedroom with Grace's perfume, to remind himself of her. When he woke in the middle of the night, for the second time, Marshal started to read a book she had recommended – *The Heart is a Lonely Hunter* – to be closer to her.

He woke up late, telling himself that the dull ache in his stomach was hunger – but it still lingered after breakfast. Marshal went for a jog, but he could not outrun the dull ache either. It stuck to him, like barnacles on the bottom of a boat, creating drag. He noted how he had forgotten about his stomach cramps, or they were absent, during his encounter with the Romanians.

Both men turned up on time, at the same time, as they met one another outside the Albert pub, on Gladstone St. It had been six months since Marshal had last seen Jack "Nails" Foster, but he appeared several years older since their previous encounter. His handlebar moustache, a hangover from his time in the special forces, had turned into an unkempt beard. His shirt and trousers looked like they had received a cursory iron, or none at all, from a cricket bat. A faded tattoo of a bulldog brandished his forearm. His skin was leathery, his eyes more red-rimmed than normal from drinking too much cheap, or expensive, whisky.

The orphan had grown up in a foster home in South Wales. The army offered him a home at seventeen, however. He joined the Paras and served in Northern Ireland in the early eighties. Foster was a good soldier who was capable of turning aggression on and off like a light switch. He knew when to follow orders – and when to interpret or ignore them. The SAS beckoned. Having conditioned himself on the Brecon Beacons for half his life, no one was surprised when the determined Para passed SAS selection. His regiment changed, but his posting didn't. Foster served in Border Country. "Shoot to kill, or don't shoot at all," was his motto. When Foster lost a couple of brothers-in-arms during the Troubles he was more determined than ever to hunt down the IRA. The terrorists. The gangsters. He would laugh – or offer up a chilling, murderous look – if anyone described the enemy as "freedom fighters". The gnarled soldier could be casually racist. But, in his defence, he could be casually sexist too. Foster turned his black, scabrous sense of humour on himself as much as others. The priapic soldier had been married two times. Once to a barmaid, once to an airline stewardess.

"I blame them for being foolish enough to marry me. But I can forgive them for being wise enough to ask for a divorce," Foster once explained to Marshal, after drinking half of bottle of *Talisker*.

The damaged soldier had a son and daughter from his first marriage. He gave his children plenty of money, but little time or affection.

Marshal was introduced to Foster through his grandfather, who also served in the Regiment. The SAS was formed from "the sweepings of the public schools and prisons." Foster came from the latter, his grandfather remarked, but was no less a soldier for it. The age gap between the two men proved no barrier for their friendship. Foster took the Para under his wing – and often took him to the pub or Special Forces Club in Knightsbridge. They were akin to each other's AA sponsor, except that when one fancied a drink then the other would be there for them by travelling to the nearest watering hole. When Foster left the army, he signed up as a mercenary – and when Marshal's contract ended out in Iraq, he joined the veteran in Somalia. The two men had drunk together, laughed together, suffered together - and killed together. On more than one occasion, Foster had called Marshal his "brother". And every six months or so the brothers caught-up with one another over a beer or two. Or ten.

Marshal noticed how his friend took a pointed look behind him, after they shook hands, before entering the pub. Foster also surveyed the patrons of the bar, casting his eye over them as if he were running a security sweep. Marshal was tempted to reassure his companion that the few people drinking at the pub during the afternoon were regulars. Jason and Michelle sat in one corner. Jason was a former signalman on the railways. His nickname would have been "sicknote", due to the amount of time he had off - if his colleagues were not scared of him. Jason now owned a fish and chip shop, as well as a few other business interests, in Uxbridge. He sometimes claimed, after a few drinks, that it was the best fish and chip shop in West London. After a few more, he might boast that it was the best in the whole of the capital. When sober, however, he would concede that it was the second best in Uxbridge. Jason would always argue, sober or otherwise, that Michelle was his better half. She had saved him from himself. Jason could grow bored easily, but he never grew bored with Michelle. They shared a similar sense of humour – and a just love of cigarettes and alcohol. Even after all these years, Michelle still looked adoringly at Jason – when she wasn't distracted by various messages on her smartphone. They were good together, greater than the sum of their parts.

Sitting down, opposite Jason and Michelle, were Terry and Chris -Elephant & Castle's answer to Gilbert and George. Both were over sixty, although their ages listed on Facebook said differently. Both were dressed in smart suits, replete with pocket squares. They sported the same Kenny Rogers beard and wore similar Yasser Arafat-like scarves decorously draped around their necks and shoulders. Terry was a renowned pantomime actor. "Oh no he isn't," his friends would joke. Chris was a lecturer at the nearby university, who toiled tirelessly in avoiding doing any real work. He licked his lips and rubbed his hands when he spoke of his imminent retirement – and securing his pension pot of gold at the end of the rainbow. They were a sweet, fun couple who finished each other's sentences and groomed one another by picking crumbs from their beards and fluff off their lapels.

Marshal bid hello to everyone and left a drink in the pump for the regulars and the staff, Molly and Kiara, who were working the day shift. Both men, out of habit or training, chose to sit with their backs to the wall. Foster glanced up and creased his brow in scrutiny every time someone entered or exited the pub. The veteran gulped down his first pint and appeared preoccupied when ordering some food. Before Marshal could ask his friend what was bothering him, he received the answer:

"This might be the last time you see me for a while, lad. I've been fucked. And not in a good way," Foster said, after Kiara served them their second pint and brought over a few non-vegetarian starters. His voice resembled a piece of bark which had been soaked in whisky for twenty years. When Foster laughed, he cackled. "Remember how I once told you about the shooting at the graveyard? Well, some fucking journalist, Hector Toynbee, got hold of a cache of documents at the Ministry of Defence and has written about it. He's outed incidents of Paras and the Regiment shooting the enemy – and named names. I read the piece of leftist propaganda. *Thatcher's Willing Executioners*. The book's not even fit to wipe my arse with. He makes a meal of Bobby Sands – and compares Martin McGuiness to Gandhi and Garibaldi, which takes the biscuit."

Marshal remembered the incident – the killing – and Foster's account of the event. It was the mid-eighties. Special Branch had heard from one of their touts. A couple of IRA foot-soldiers were due to drive at night to an old cemetery, just outside of Ballymena, to collect a cache of Armalite rifles hidden in an empty grave. Foster was part of the SAS squad tasked with staking out the graveyard. Halfway through the night the two IRA operatives turned up in a battered Land Rover. The squad's orders were to apprehend the enemy and avoid engagement if possible. The operatives could prove a valuable source of intelligence. The threat of prison, coupled with financial incentives, could turn even the most fanatical Provo into a compliant informer.

Foster was charged to break cover and confront the enemy, bellowing out instructions for the two men to drop any weapons and raise their hands. It was dark. Thick cloud smothered out the moonlight. Patrick Toohey, the senior of the two IRA operatives, let off a couple of rounds from a Browning pistol and retreated towards the Land Rover, in hope of making his escape. Foster's colleagues gave chase. The overweight Toohey became breathless, or fell over, before reaching the vehicle. He dropped his weapon and surrendered. In the meantime, Foster repeated his order for the second IRA operative, Finn Mullen, to relinquish his weapon. In the darkness, the shovel Mullen was carrying resembled a rifle. He turned towards the British soldier, still holding the spade in two hands, at waist level. Foster opened fire. Three rounds to the chest. Shoot to kill, or don't shoot at all.

It turned out that Finn Mullen was only sixteen years old – and the eldest child of John Mullen, an IRA Brigade Commander. The rabble-rousing Mullen – he had once been called, as a compliment or otherwise, a "Catholic Reverend Paisley" – demanded justice. Two days after the killing at the graveyard a Paratrooper was gunned down outside a pub, as the young recruit was making his way back to the barracks. Officially Mullen denied any involvement in the reprisal killing. Unofficially, he boasted that the murder would just be the start of a bloodbath.

The authorities conducted an investigation into the events at the cemetery. The unnamed soldier was exonerated, and it was judged to be a just killing. Information was leaked to the press, pre-empting the official findings. Finn Mullen had been carrying a Webley pistol in his waistband at the time of his death. Ballistics linked the pistol to the murder of an RUC officer, from a year previous. Also, a week before the shooting, it was reported that Finn Mullen, along with four other friends, had assaulted a Protestant youth and gang-raped his girlfriend.

Initially Patrick Toohey testified that the soldiers were aware that his friend was unarmed. They were just on a drunken night out, looking to scare each other. "We just wanted to see what a dead body looked like," Toohey protested, somewhat ironically. He soon changed his testimony, however, when confronted with evidence which contradicted his statement.

John Mullen purchased a new black, solemn suit and went before the cameras, claiming that the British were guilty of covering up their war crimes. The soldier was guilty of murdering his son in cold blood. Executing him. "My baby boy did not own a gun. It was a plant… Patrick Toohey's testimony was coerced. Or a deal was done. His sentence will be reduced. I guarantee it. It was an unlawful killing, by an unlawful occupying force... My son was an altar boy, a wee angel. He was a good Catholic, but being a good Catholic seems to be a crime in this country... There should be a public trial, not some farce of an enquiry behind closed doors where students get to mark their own homework. The truth must out. Murder will out. These special forces dogs have been let off the leash and given a licence to kill... I deserve to know the name of the man who butchered my flesh and blood. No name, no justice. No name, no justice."

John Mullen was interviewed by a host of newspapers and took to the airwaves, to lobby the authorities to release the name of the soldier. A group of Labour Party MPs raised urgent questions in parliament to support the campaign. The tragedy, if it could have been called such, made John Mullen a household name. The press soon spoke of a triumvirate of Adams, McGuiness and Mullen. Marshal considered how Mullen would have been the Lepidus of the three. But the army closed ranks and refused to cave into pressure from the media to disclose the name and review their policies.

Several years ago, over a few drinks, poolside at a villa in Malaga, Foster offered up his version of events to Marshal:

"I was ninety percent sure that he was carrying a shovel. But the light, or darkness, can play tricks on you. I was not about to let the bastard shoot at me, or one of my brothers... I knew, having heard his voice, that he was young. But a sixteen-year-old killer is still a killer. There were few innocents during the Troubles. You were more likely to find a leprechaun walking the streets of Belfast, shopping for a lid for his pot of gold... There isn't a soldier I know who wouldn't have made the same choice. You know the score. Kill or be killed."

Marshal appreciated his friend's jokes about Sands and McGuiness, but he refrained from laughing. The issue of a journalist exposing various British soldiers was serious. Deadly serious. Names were redacted or changed for a reason in reports, which covered shooting incidents during the Troubles. The peace agreement in Northern Ireland did not mean that all participants, on both sides, were keen on forgiving and forgetting.

"Mullen may have crossed the floor, from terrorist to politician, since the Good Friday agreement - but he will still be baying for my blood. I would be the same if I found out that he shot my boy. Mullen says he's not linked to any paramilitary organisations anymore, but he's still close to the IRA, like white on rice. I'd prefer not to be in that bastard's crosshairs. Some oik at the MOD called me, after the book had been out for a week, to say that "the publication might be cause for concern." No shit, Sherlock. Apparently, the MOD are intending to sue the publishers and have them remove the book from publication. But the horse has already bolted – and could trample me underfoot. I've not been this worried since I was waiting on my last divorce settlement," Foster remarked, although even his black sense of humour failed to lighten his mood. "I always suspected that my past might catch up with me. I don't regret getting blood on my hands. It was either them or us. But I did some things that I would rather not tell my children about. Not that they must think much of their father anyway... Border Country was like the Wild West, back then. We were the cowboys, and they were the Indians - except that instead of carrying bows and arrows they were armed with Armalite rifles and Semtex."

"Are you okay? Do you need help with anything?" Marshal asked, perturbed by how his friend's past had caught up with him and turned his world upside down. He recognised his friend's anxious look. He had seen it, in the mirror. Marshal had looked over his shoulder, more than once, after dealing with the Albanians. If any of the remaining members of the gang had found out that Marshal had been responsible for assassinating the enforcer Viktor Baruti and planting weapons in the club they worked out of, the Albanians would have hunted Marshal down and killed him without hesitation. There were days, during the first couple of months after taking out his enemy, when Marshal carried his Glock 21 around with him. He was marginally more worried about encountering his enemy than Grace finding the weapon on his person or in his flat. The ex-soldier felt like he was conducting an illicit affair with the gun at times.

"No, I am fine on that front. But I appreciate the offer. Your grandfather would be proud of you. You're a good lad. For all of the bravado around not one step back and no retreat, no surrender, I've decided to disappear. Better to be safe than sorry. A friend of mine has offered me use of his villa in Portugal. Perhaps I'll finally bow to the inevitable and take up golf. The plan will be to find a senorita to put up with me enough during the night so that she will stay and cook me breakfast in the morning. I will also get in touch sooner or later and invite you and Grace over. We both know how dull peace and retirement are. I would rather get shot than die of boredom. Or if you visit without Grace, you could have even more fun."

"I am a changed man, Jack. Although I am unsure if I have changed for the better," Marshal replied.

"Surely you must have strayed and had at least one affair to keep you happy, if you have stayed with Grace this long?" Foster asked, in slight disbelief. The soldier even paused when bringing his pint glass up to his lips. He knew Marshal, he went through relationships like the MOD went through budgets, from overspending on consultants. It was not just due to the drink that Foster had got the names of Marshal's girlfriends wrong in the past, after being introduced to them. They changed with the seasons. His young friend once said that he was more likely to meet Elvis than Miss Right.

"To my shame, I have been as faithful as a Jihad and as reliable as a Kalashnikov."

"I can think of worse fates than being married to a fashion model. And who am I to give expert advice on love and relationships? I can offer you some valuable advice on pre-nups now, though. But don't let my experiences, or those of others, put you off taking things forward with Grace."

"They won't," Marshal said, lying. How long would it be before he cheated on Grace, after they were married? Man was not the most naturally constant creature in the animal kingdom. *We are arrant knaves, all. Get thee to a nunnery. Why would'st thou be a breeder of sinners?* How long before he grew so distant, that she could not recognise him anymore? How long before Grace found his gun? The honeymoon period always comes before the marriage. Before each marriage, Foster had promised that he would be a good husband, that he would change his ways. Marshal remembered how one of his friends in the army, Percy Norton, had slept with one of the hotel receptionists the night after his wedding. At the time, Marshal did not know whether to admire the Guards officer or be appalled by him. Everything is born to die, including relationships. Marshal remembered how his mother and father's marriage had ended. His mother's expression was uncommonly serene when she received the last rites. Marshal's boyish face was contorted in pain, his fists clenched in anger. He had felt so much torment because he had felt so much love. It was tantamount to a mathematical equation. Marshal later concluded that if you did not invest yourself in a relationship then you could avoid becoming bankrupt when things collapsed.

Either he was suffering from indigestion, or the dull ache in Marshal's stomach had returned.

4.

Both men ordered the steak for lunch. Not wishing to discuss Albanians, IRA terrorists or failed relationships any longer, Marshal and Foster joined Jason and Michelle for a drink after their meal.

"What did you do in the navy?" Foster asked, after being introduced to the regular.

"I mainly played rugby and broke up, or started, various barfights down in Plymouth. What did you do in the army?"

"I made a killing," the ex-special forces soldier remarked, with a twinkle in his eye and a whisky tumbler in his hand. Rather than being an occupational hazard during his career, there were occasions when the soldier considered that killing was a perquisite to the job. Some people deserved to die, he judged.

Marshal and Foster had a couple of cigarettes outside and then said their goodbyes. The old friends didn't look back as they strolled off in opposite directions. They also both failed to look across the road and notice a couple of youths sitting on a bench, eating their lunch whilst keeping a covert eye on the veteran soldier. The youths - Connor and Sinead - held hands like lovers as they walked down the street, following Foster. But they were brother and sister, the niece and nephew of Sean Duggan.

Marshal smoked another cigarette. Ironically, the smoke felt purifying. He briefly closed his eyes in satisfaction, imagining he was elsewhere. The streets were crowded, the noise deafening. Too many people were saying too many inane things on their mobile phones. Too many people were dressed in ill-judged vest tops. There were too many cyclists, with garish shorts and even louder opinions, riding past – usually through red lights. Marshal fancied that they were even more self-righteous than a Liberal Democrat - if that was at all possible.

Marshal put on his headphones and turned up the music which he had downloaded onto his smart phone. Dylan, again.

"It's now or never More than ever
When I met you, I didn't think you would do
It's soon after midnight
And I don't want nobody but you."

He welcomed the message from Grace as he walked home. She was an island of something in an ocean of nothingness.

Have just landed. I am going to pop by the bookshop and see Emma to catch-up, before getting to you. I hope you had a nice lunch with Jack – and it wasn't just a liquid lunch. How are you?

Marshal replied:

My heart's aching for you of course, but it's a welcome distraction from my burgeoning sore head.

Another odious cyclist ran through a red light. An odorous traffic warden spat out gum, striking the calf of an elderly woman walking in front of him.

Grace replied:

The skirt I am wearing will distract you even more, I imagine. Get some sleep. Do not worry about cooking dinner later. We can eat out. Love you. Xx

Grace had first uttered those two words several months ago. They had just had sex. Trust, intimacy and lust had ebbed through their limbs, fingertips and mouths. They were breathless. Chests rose and fell in unison. Her hair and skin smelled better than cigarettes or cask strength whisky. Grace had given something of herself, more than just her sinuous body. Her head lay on Marshal's left breast, their legs entwined. Her fingers played with the cross around her neck.

"Despite all the gossip on websites and photos of me walking out of restaurants with various actors and celebrities, I have not been with many men. Most of those dates were set up by publicists as photo opportunities. We acted shocked and that we craved privacy, but the press were tipped off as to where we would be. If you define those stunts as dates, then I have probably dated more gay than straight men over the years. Actors can be even more self-obsessed than fashion models. I was a trophy, an ornament, on a professional or personal level, when I lived in New York. I was living in a beautiful bubble, a gilded cage. My career was everything, I told myself. But it was nothing too. I had to smile so much at parties that the corners of my mouth began to ache. Some men want to possess women. Their idea of romance is to put a line of coke on a glass table and then ask you to dress up as a secretary or schoolgirl. Once isn't enough. It's too much. We all seem to play a part in life. All the world's a stage. But I can be myself when I'm with you, James," Grace remarked, her voice a mixture of vulnerability and candour, her eyes glistening with tears. But not tears of sorrow. "I feel free. You make me laugh. I am not sure if I have ever been happier. I love my home, I love my bookshop, and I love you. I must sound foolish."

"Socialists are foolish. Extinction Rebellion protesters are foolish. Bono is foolish. You're not foolish," Marshal replied, drily and reassuringly.

The following day, when out together for lunch in central London, the couple approached Westminster Cathedral in Victoria. Marshal remembered how Grace told him, after only knowing him a few days, that he should enter the next Catholic church he encountered, instead of just passing by. It would be good for his soul. He took her by the hand, and they entered behind a gaggle of American tourists. Grace genuflected in a floral, summer dress. He bent his knee too. Submitting. The smell of incense was still familiar from when he was a boy and attended mass. The decorative marbles were bold but elegant. Shafts of sunlight expunged most, but not all, of the gloom. Remarkably, the tourists failed to annoy him. Marshal paused before each stone image of the Stations of the Cross. Melancholy and reverent. The statues and images of Christ seemed to follow him around the chamber. He wanted to feel God. Fill a grave-sized hole. While Grace visited the giftshop Marshal found a quiet corner, knelt, bowed his head, clasped his perspiring hands together and prayed, like a ring rusty boxer. Guilt washed over him, at first. He was a sinner, like the next man. Like every man. The soldier asked for God's forgiveness, as though He still existed. His feelings of guilt were still stronger than those of absolution, however. Marshal also spoke to his mother, as if she still existed. He believed that she would have liked Grace. He joked to himself that he felt like he had just been in a therapy session, except that God did not charge by the hour. Marshal wiped the tears from his eyes and steadied himself as he got to his feet. Grace pretended that she had not noticed Marshal praying. Her bronze skin glowed in the candlelight. Holy and beautiful. They unwittingly came together at the end of the aisle of pews, as if they were a bride and groom.

"I stupidly forgot to say this last night. I love you too," Marshal sweetly remarked – and meant it.

Love was nourishment for the soul. Love was evidence of the existence of the soul. But the word could also sit like a stone tablet on Marshal's chest. He found it hard but not impossible to love, like his stomach found it hard but not impossible to break down the steak he had eaten for lunch. He was outside, but still he felt like the walls were closing in. His thumb hovered over the buttons of his Blackberry, seemingly frozen. His skin felt flushed, like his blood wanted to escape from every pore.

He was on the cusp of being out of breath. But then he nearly laughed at himself – and breathed out. He thought how he had not even suffered a panic attack when under fire in Helmand. Marshal also pictured Grace's eyes, which were a window into her kind, Catholic soul. Grace was proof of God's existence.

Marshal replied:

Love you too. Xx

Motes of dust swirled around in the room like insects. Marshal pulled the curtains across. The light began to hurt his eyes - drill into his pupils. He poured himself a brandy and swished the elixir around in a special glass Grace had bought for him. She arranged for it to be engraved. *"When you're going through hell, keep going. Winston Churchill."* He switched on the television to take a cursory look at the news, but quickly turned it off. Marshal did not quite know what made him more nauseous, the news or the newsreaders. The world was going to hell in a handcart still. He did not expect anything else. He closed his eyes and sank deeper into the chair, but sleep was still proving elusive. He picked up a book from the coffee table. There was a pile of half a dozen hardbacks and paperbacks, fiction and non-fiction. The titles included Max Hasting's *Armageddon*, Roger Moorhouse's *The Devil's Alliance*, Jane Austen's *Emma* and Richard Foreman's *Jerusalem: Kingdom of Heaven*. Marshal selected the following: *Russian Roulette: The Life and Times of Graham Greene*, by Richard Greene. A quote from *The Quiet American* leapt from the page and fleetingly increased his sore head and tightened the small knot in his stomach. *"Sooner or later, one has to take sides. If one is to remain human."* The usually voracious reader soon found it difficult to concentrate – and he put the book down.

Marshal felt a calling. He covered the kitchen table with newspaper and cleaned his gun. With Grace spending more time at his flat, he was mindful that he might not be able to attend to the Glock for a while. It was good that Grace was living with him more. But it wasn't all good. Nothing is all good. Including God. He sometimes liked to have the flat all to himself. Do nothing and sleep. Turn himself into a block of stone. Feel nothing. Drink. Get lost in a novel. Remember or forget Helmand. Smoke with the window closed. He liked to leave the house and not tell anyone when he would be back. He sometimes liked unemptied ashtrays and not placing his glass on a coaster. He liked filling the wine rack with bottles of vodka and whisky. The ex-Para did not want his life to feel regimented, like he was back in the army again.

He checked his watch, a silver *Breitling Chronomat*. It was a Christmas present from Grace. She had engraved the back, with a quote from Coleridge.

"To be beloved is all I need
And whom I love, I love indeed."

Marshal opened all the windows - and cooked some bacon - in order to oust out any lingering smell of gun oil in the air. He tidied the flat, ready for Grace's arrival, and finally fell asleep.

5.

His fellow republican – and rival – Gerry Adams started to call himself the "Big Lad" in the seventies, partly because Michael Collins had been known as the "Big Fella". And so, not to feel he was being left behind, Mullen demanded that those under his command named him the "Big Man".

Mullen sat at his large mahogany desk, at his office on the top floor of a plush complex in Mornington Crescent. The Irish MP resembled a less avuncular Brendan Gleeson – with greyer hair and glassier eyes. His combover did its best to disguise his thinning hair. But its best wasn't good enough. He had once been told that the only true cure for baldness was castration. But it was the only price that was not worth paying for getting his hair back. Diamond studded cufflinks peeped out of sleeves. The cuffs covered a *Cartier* watch, a present from Aung Sang Suu Kyi. Mullen wore an expensive Savile Row suit, which had fitted better a year ago. Muscle had turned to flab over the years, although he could still appear physically intimidating. When he snarled and snorted, Mullen still resembled a bull of a man. He confessed to have been living "the good life" over the past decade or so. He no longer had to hunker down in safe houses, eating baked beans or watery Irish stew. His chubby digits looked like uncooked sausages. His index finger could barely fit through the trigger guard of an old Browning pistol he still owned.

Two colour photos – one of his mother and daughter, the other of his deceased son – stood on the left side of his desk. On the other side stood two faded black and white photographs. The first was of Colm Mullen, a republican legend - arrested and executed for leading a campaign to bomb police stations and hospitals in London during the second half of the nineteenth century. The second was of Liam Mullen, John's grandfather. Liam Mullen was part of a delegation which met with senior members of the Third Reich during the Second World War. The plan was to put the Irish state at Hitler's disposal, to have the British fight on another front and weaken their position. Many Irish were ashamed and condemnatory of Eamon de Valera's actions, that he went too far. For Liam Mullen, however, de Valera did not go far enough in aiding the Nazis against their common enemy. After the war, Liam would spit every time he had to mention de Valera and lament missed opportunities. "Better Hitler and the Germans, than Churchill and the British," he would pugnaciously argue.

A computer, ashtray and large measure of *Bushmills* were also regular features on the desk – as well as a few boxes of pills. Metformin, for his diabetes. Warfarin, which helped thin his blood to prevent strokes. And Viagra.

The sound of the air conditioning hummed in the background. The bulletproof glass blocked out the noise of the busy street below.

A colourful landscape by Jack Yeats hung above a *Terence Conran* leather sofa. Mullen was not particularly fond of the artwork. Although he did appreciate that he had purchased the investment as a tax write-off. On the wall opposite the sofa were rows of photographs, hung at eye level, of Mullen pictured with the good and great, often shaking hands or embracing. The Clintons, Angela Merkel, Bob Geldof, Nicolas Sarkozy, Neil Kinnock, Bono, Tony Blair, and Donald Tusk hung side by side, like a well-attired version of a rogue's gallery. Occasionally a space would open-up on the pale blue wall, as a photo was removed. But the photos of Brian Epstein and Lance Armstrong were soon replaced by shots taken with other celebrities and statespersons. Mullen boasted that a picture of Thatcher was conspicuous by its absence, explaining that he had refused to be photographed with her - although the truth was that Thatcher had denied his request to be snapped with the terrorist.

John Mullen pursed his lips and tapped his foot beneath the desk, as he stared at the burner phone. Waiting for it to chime.

Nolan needed to call soon, he impatiently thought. He would be called downstairs within the hour, to give a talk in the conference space of the building to a group of business leaders. Mullen would give his usual spiel about conciliation not conflict, choosing the future over the past. Despite having given the lecture a hundred times before, Mullen had the gift of oratory and could make it sound fresh and sincere. His audience would believe that he had composed the speech just for them - they had after all paid him extra to deliver an original lecture. The fee had been paid – and they would not dare ask for their money back. Mullen took part in at least four speaking engagements each month. As much as crime paid, as much as terrorism had paid, Mullen still needed additional, legitimate, revenue streams to fund his lifestyle. His wife – and mistress – did not come cheap, unfortunately. Similarly, the lawyers he retained wanted their pound of flesh and his staff costs, those officially on his books and those who worked for him more informally, were a weeping sore on his finances.

There was another reason, aside from the fee, why Mullen was keen to honour the engagement. It would provide him with an alibi. After the event he would take a few of the participants for drinks at a nearby hotel, where he would drink until the bar closed and stay the night. He would call room service in the dead of night and be first downstairs for breakfast in the morning, appearing on the CCTV cameras of the establishment. He would be accompanied by his Head of Security, Sean Duggan.

Duggan sat on the sofa in the office, watching Ireland play Wales in a friendly rugby game. The sound was on mute, so as not to disturb his boss. The match was close. Too close. The Irish should have sewn things up by now. They were their own worst enemies, sometimes.

There should be no such fucking thing as a friendly.

He blamed the English on the coaching staff. His features were as hard, but not as smooth, as marble. His gnarled eyes were a window into his thuggish soul. From a distance it appeared like Duggan possessed a Kirk Douglas-like cleft chin. But on closer inspection it was a scar, from a broken bottle during a bar fight. Duggan often dreamed of one day encountering the Protestant bastard who had inflicted the injury during his youth. He would not just cut his chin open. Rather, he would cut open the whole of his enemy, from his face down to his groin. Mullen's lieutenant had taken off his suit jacket, exposing the shoulder holster he wore, containing a well-maintained Sig Sauer P220. Duggan ran his knuckle-scarred hands through his short, bristling red hair. He was anxious, either for the rugby game or that Nolan had yet to call. Part of him wanted to oversee the operation this evening. He wanted to be the one to pull the trigger. The fifty-odd year old wanted to kill again. Feel alive. The war was not over. Every Para and SAS butcher deserved to die, as far as the freedom fighter was concerned. Foster was a modern Black and Tan. He wore the same uniform as those who had interned his kinsmen. Duggan would have to be content with just forming, rather than executing, his plan. He understood Mullen's desire for him to have an alibi too.

Mullen checked his personal phone, which he had put on silent. He had received two calls from his wife, Mary, and one call from his daughter, Teresa. He had no urge to speak to his long-suffering – and long suffered – wife. His wife had turned into his mother-in-law over the past few years. Part shrew, part religious nutcase. She spent half of her time in church – and the other half complaining or shopping. His wife was one of the reasons why he spent so much time in London. Mullen would have divorced her, if not for the frightening expense of it all. He no longer could stomach sleeping in the same bed with "bony, bitter hag" when he was home. Mary failed to raise a smile, or anything else, when Mullen thought of his wife.

"I can't fuck her, I can't divorce her, and I can't kill her. I can ignore the bint, though," he had remarked to Duggan, the day before, when she called him then.

Mullen was in no mood to speak to his daughter, either. She would only chew his ear off about not calling his wife enough. Teresa always took her mother's side, except when she needed to ask for money.

His mistress, Josephine, had also sent him a text, accompanied by a photo of her wearing a new lingerie set she had just bought in *Selfridge's* (or rather he had just bought in *Selfridge's*). She wanted to know if Mullen wanted to visit her this evening. The former escort, who the politician had seen on and off for five years, had retired (she said). In return for putting her on the payroll as a parliamentary assistant, Josephine had agreed to be his full-time mistress.

Duggan sniffed. Mullen glanced at his old friend, narrowing his cold eyes in scrutiny, or accusation. Had he innocently sniffed, or had he just snorted some coke during his recent trip to the toilet? Mullen had warned his Head of Security about drug-taking while on duty. Duggan needed a clear head, especially tonight. The loyal lieutenant had kept his word to not snort anything while on duty. A promise was a promise. He did, however, rub some coke into his gums in the toilet to help take the edge of things.

Duggan refrained from saying anything, partly because the phone finally rang. The old man's heart skipped a beat, as if he were a teenager again and a girl was calling. Mullen wiped his perspiring palm against his trouser leg and answered the burner, putting the call on speaker phone. He was only expecting to receive one call on the device.

"We're ready," a deep, guttural, Northern Irish voice intoned. "Do you want us to take him?"

It was now, or potentially never. Their fish could slip through the net - if they failed to gaff him immediately.

Mullen glanced at Duggan, who nodded. The father of the murdered teenager would have proceeded even without agreement of his lieutenant.

"Do it," he ordered, his ruddy face screwed-up in unbridled malevolence. His lips receded, revealing swollen gums and coffee-stained teeth. Mullen's hand gripped the whiskey tumbler tightly, as if it were about to shatter. Conflict over conciliation. The past, not the future. Justice and resentment laced his words, like the finest of poisons. They were one in the same thing. Semi-divine.

Mullen's own phone lit-up again, with another message from his mistress. She asked again whether he would like to see her that evening.

Without irony, he replied:
Not tonight, Josephine.

Marshal woke and rehydrated. He checked his phone and opened a message from Grace. She apologised for running late and said she would meet him at the restaurant. Marshal showered, put on one of his few remaining shirts which didn't smell of cigarette smoke, and headed out.

Bobo Social. It was not just the best restaurant in the area because it was the only restaurant in the area. The establishment managed to combine a relaxed, cordial atmosphere with old-fashioned service. Good produce was cooked well at a not over-inflated price. A bar, renowned for its cocktails, sat at the heart of a dozen or so tables, occupied by couples, families and groups of friends. The aromas emanating from the open kitchen at the rear were suitably moreish. The ribeye on the menu was a match, in size and flavour, for any found at an Argentinian steakhouse. A simple omelette was cooked with skill and love. Marshal was a regular and greeted, with or nod or handshake, several fellow diners. Taj and Richard ordered another cocktail each, still raising a glass to a Conservative majority (albeit the party would always be too centrist for their liking). Oliver Webb-Carter, the editor of the magazine *Aspects of History*, was working his way through the latest Bernard Cornwell novel and a large gin and tonic. He was waiting for his wife, Marjan – whose idea of turning up on time rivalled Blucher's. Jeremy Knight, the owner of *Hej*, a local coffeeshop, was enjoying something stronger than coffee. For a misanthrope, Marshal could be remarkably gregarious. He was also familiar with the staff and a few of them came over, throughout the evening, to say hello. There was the general manager Yoann, a Frenchman who was thankfully not too French. Patricia, or Pati, greeted people at the door – with a consummate sense of elegance and professionalism. Izzy, though only twenty-two, wore more knitwear than a great-aunt. She was never happy until her customers were. Towards the end of the night the chef, Monsur, also popped over to see Marshal. Partly he wanted to check that everything was fine with the food, but more so he wanted to ask his friend when they were next going out for a beer and curry. Monsur was an experienced chef, who still retained a youthful enthusiasm for cooking. He knew his eggs, Cacklebean or otherwise. He preferred to inspire fear rather than affection in his team – and would sometimes gaze out from the kitchen like the Great Eye of Sauron, seeing everything. His standards were as high as his blood pressure – and his jokes as coarse as the pate.

Marshal sat at the bar, a cross between Norm and Frasier, and had a drink with Jeremy while he waited for Grace. And she was worth the wait. Even after a year Grace could still make him go weak at the knees – and compel Marshal to stand-up ramrod straight and puff out his chest as if he were a proud recruit on his first parade. Pati showed the couple to their table. Marshal was initially speechless as he drank in the sight of the former model and breathed in her perfume. Eventually he embraced and kissed her, nearly tripping over a chair before doing so. Her features were sharp and soft, strong yet feminine. Her hair had grown fairer, her complexion more sun-kissed, during the summer. She was dressed in a white, *Claudie Pierlot* sleeveless midi dress. She looked good in white. But Grace could even look stylish in mismatched pyjamas – and White Reeboks – Marshal judged. The famed model was classically, symmetrically, elegantly attractive – yet Marshal liked the way Grace looked when she cocked her head to one side when reading, scrunching her features in curiosity or amusement. Marshal sometimes thought Grace looked like an English Faith Hill or Miranda Lambert. She resembled Gwyneth Paltrow in *Emma* and *Shakespeare in Love* – rather than the figure who now pedalled silly beauty treatments and other hokum. But, more than anyone else, Grace Wilde was Grace Wilde. She was too beautiful for him. Too good for him, he thought. There were not many things in the world that were worth getting up in the morning for after turning forty. But Grace was one of them.

Marshal ordered a bottle of the Malbec. He promised himself that he would not drink too much though. He wanted to be largely sober when he got home. He wanted to remember making love to Grace. A brief silence hung in the air, like the smell of perfume, after the waitress left. The couple shared a moment. For once they did not need to force a smile. Music played in the background. Phil Collins was on, again. Chef was a fan.

"If this world makes you crazy
And you've taken all you can bear
Just call me up
Because you know I'll be there."

Part of Marshal felt prompted to blurt out how much he missed and wanted her. Loved her. That he had even thought about marrying her. He wanted to unburden himself to Grace about his frustration at not being able to help Jack. There were so many important things – secrets and lies – that he had failed to share with Grace. If she knew him, would she still love him? Confession was supposed to be good for the soul. He took a breath and spoke, appearing a little vulnerable. There was a moment when Grace thought he might say something profound or important. But the moment vanished.

"How are things at the shop?"

"Sales are fine. I may even be able to afford to order some non-house wine tonight," Grace wryly replied. As much as it had been a dream for the model to open a bookshop, and she was fine for money, she still wanted to run a profitable business. "We are hosting a launch party for a bestselling historian in a fortnight's time. Although every author seems to put "bestselling" in front of their name now. I thought you might like to attend. I may need rescuing from a lecherous literary agent or, worse, a champagne socialist."

The thought of having to engage with the chattering classes made Marshal's teeth itch, but he agreed to come to the event. He had been a pillar of support of the bookshop - and Grace - over the past year. The keen reader was a sounding board for Grace's ideas - and had even worked a few shifts in the shop to help-out. The best and worst part of working at the bookshop, for Marshal, was dealing with the customers.

"How was your trip?"

"I didn't do too much, but it still felt exhausting – and not just because of the jetlag. I felt like I was through the looking glass, viewing my past, at times. I stayed with Ophelia. She had to work a couple of shoots. I accompanied her on one of the days. The agents are still the hardest working drug dealers in the industry, preferring their clients to pop pills rather than eat. Over reliance on medication is preferable to being overweight. Cocaine is less calorific than chocolate. The fashion photographers are still misogynists or perverts. The designers screech rather than talk. The trade is a circus, populated by clowns and a few ringmasters. At least time spent on the photoshoot reminded me why I retired," Grace remarked, wistfully. "I feel like a princess – locked up in a tower of a Manhattan high-rise. Any prince I kiss will turn into a frog," Ophelia confided in her friend, world weary behind a mask of pristine make-up. The uptown girl had yet to find her backstreet guy.

An idle thought struck Marshal while Grace was talking. Modelling was a little like soldiering. The long hours took a toll on the body and soul. You had to follow orders that you were not always comfortable with. You needed to watch your weight. *Models possess looks that can kill. Soldiers carry automatic weapons.*

Grace went on to speak about the latest production of *The Cherry Orchard* she saw on Broadway, and the restaurants she visited. The best part of the trip was coming home, however.

"And have you been eating properly while I've been away?" Grace asked, with a raised eyebrow and slight maternal look of scrutiny and rebuke. She expected to find a few takeaway boxes in the bin when she got back to the flat.

"Well, I have been attempting to order the right wine to accompany each relevant dish, if that's what you mean," Marshal playfully replied.

The candle on the table glowed in front of Grace, illuminating her amused, striking expression. Marshal realised that if he could spend the remainder of his life with anyone – grow old with them – it would be Grace. She understood and appreciated him, at least that part of him which he allowed the world to see.

"You've cut your hand," Grace suddenly remarked, noticing the small scab on his knuckle.

"I accidentally scraped it against a brick wall when I was walking home the other evening. Thankfully, the alcohol helped numbed the pain," Marshal said, the soul of nonchalance. He did not always feel comfortable lying to Grace, but he also knew he was good at it.

Phil Collins played on. It could have been worse, Marshal fancied. Chef could have been a fan of Will Young.

After their main courses – Marshal had the skate wing and Grace the salmon – the owner of Bobo, Mike Benson, came over to join two of his favourite regular customers. Mike stood at just 5.5 but he walked tall. The staff were split 50/50 as to whether he wore lifts or not in his shoes. He worked hard and smart – and was justly proud of the business he had created. His accent betrayed how the restaurateur was born in Wales – and had worked in France and South Africa over the years. Marshal admired how his friend was able to juggle all his work and family commitments, whilst still keeping a hand on a pint glass when needed. He was good company. Self-confident, but self-deprecating too. Mike was the only person Marshal knew who owned a more extensive collection of books on the Third Reich than him – although Marshal didn't quite know if that was a good thing or not.

"How are things?" Marshal asked, after inviting Mike to sit at their table.

With the subtlest nod of his head the restaurant owner communicated to the waitress, Sara, to pour him a large glass of Rioja – and to give the diners he sat with a drink on the house.

"It's another day in paradise," Mike joked, rolling his eyes, making reference to the Phil Collins song playing in the background and Chef's unhealthy obsession with the singer.

"Business is good it seems," Grace commented, surveying the bustling establishment. All the tables were full inside and plenty of people were taking advantage of the fine weather and sipping (or gulping down) cocktails outside.

"Aye, against all odds," Mike said, as the next song started. "I spent the afternoon with my accountant. Tax really is a four-letter word – and not just for dyslexics. Government assistance! The term could be one of your oxymorons, James."

Marshal was tempted to stay for a few drinks with Mike – and Chef offered to make the couple something special for dessert – but Grace was a greater temptation and sweeter than anything he could cook-up. He shared a look with her. They may have been a little tired, but they were more than a little amorous too.

Despite his keenness to get home, Marshal avoided the less scenic shortcut he had taken the previous evening. They were barely through the door to his flat when he kissed her deeply and began to take off her dress, breathing in Grace's fragrance like incense. There were times when she surrendered to him, and times when she took command. For once, the soldier was fine about following orders.

A cooling breeze began to temper the balmy evening. The moon hung in the air, like long-term service medal. Grace fell asleep shortly after making love. Her body was soft, yet also firm, against his. Her arm was draped across his chest. Usually, her skin felt as smooth as silk, but her forearm was covered in goosepimples. He would have been happy to kiss every last one.

With other women, Marshal had felt like they were somehow intruding, outstaying their welcome, after staying over for more than five nights. But he had been happy for Grace to make herself at home. He would even encourage her to stay and fix her breakfast - or invite her for a coffee at *Hej*. She had spent an increasing amount of time living at the flat during the past year. She hinted how she would be fine to downsize and live south of the river. It was as if they were already married, or certainly engaged. But Grace desired and deserved more. The sacrament of marriage may be a lie – but it was a good, beautiful, and honourable lie. Especially compared with most of the other delusions out there in the world, Marshal judged.

All he could hear was her breathing. There were no distant sirens or late-night revellers on the street outside. All was well. Grace's fingers briefly twitched, as if calling out to him. Marshal thought about where he might be able to buy an engagement ring.

6.

Morning.

Lemony sunshine squeezed its way through the curtains. It would be another day gilded with fine weather. Marshal and Grace made love again, with carnality and consideration, stretching out their tired limbs. The dull ache in his stomach returned afterwards, even before he smoked his first cigarette. They then went for a coffee in *Hej*.

When they got back to the flat, Grace explained how she needed to travel home to attend to various things.

"I will be back later. Let's have a nice evening in tonight," Grace suggested, after booking a taxi. The model had spent half her life as a wallflower at endless parties and restaurants. She preferred to spend a large part of the second half at home, with Marshal. And, though she did not openly mention it to him yet, with a family.

"Would like me to cook something?"

"I thought I said I would like a nice evening," Grace mischievously countered, much to the relief of both their tastebuds and digestive systems. "Have a good day. Have you got anything planned for this afternoon?"

"I'll be busy doing nothing in some fashion, I imagine."

Marshal thought he may watch another season of *Dexter*, finish off a novel or go for a run. He also had a mind to buy a copy of *Thatcher's Willing Executioners*, as much as it might vex the ex-Para to read it. There was also the option to decamp onto a bar stall for part of the afternoon, have a nap and then wait for Grace to return.

Marshal received the call shortly after midday. It was the police. In a voice which tried to blend sombreness with authoritarianism, the officer asked Marshal to confirm his identity – and if he knew a "Mr John Foster". A flicker of confusion initially marked his expression. Marshal never knew that his friend's real name was John. "John" had been found murdered that morning. Marshal gunned out a couple of questions, but the officer remarked that they would give out what information they could when Marshal met his colleague, one Detective Inspector Martin Coulson, at the nearby police station on Manor Place.

Marshal had paced up and down his living room during his phone call but when he hung-up he fell into a chair, fearing that his legs might give way. He wanted to be sick. Bile, sorrow or something else was lodged in his throat like a cricket ball which he had swallowed but couldn't digest. If he was sober, he wanted to be drunk. If drunk, he wanted to be sober. He pictured his friend, cackling after telling a ribald story. But the image was, at best, bittersweet. Marshal also recalled the moment when Foster had likely saved his life. They had been serving on a tanker, off the coast of Somalia. A couple of boats, containing a dozen Somali pirates, pulled alongside their vessel. Bullets pinged against the tanker, as Marshal and his fellow PMCs returned fire. A pirate unleashed a volley which crept upwards against the hull and would have cut Marshal in half, but Foster predicted the trajectory of the gunfire and pulled his friend out of the way. The SAS veteran noted the scrawny, khat-chewing young pirate who had nearly killed his friend – and emptied half a magazine into the enemy. Shoot to kill, or don't shoot at all.

Marshal's hand shook as he held the remote control and switched on the news. Details were sketchy or absent. The internet furnished him with a few more details and photographs, which he stared at whilst wishing he could unsee things too. His soul felt like sludge. Marshal poured himself a whisky and lit a cigarette to help calm his nerves, but they felt like placebos.

Foster's corpse had been dumped on Herbert Crescent in Knightsbridge, outside the Special Forces Club, during the early hours of the morning. Photos downloaded onto various news and social media outlets, which annoyingly Marshal had to sign-up to, showed how his friend was still dressed in his trousers from yesterday, but his feet and torso were bare and bloody. His face was barely recognisable. Swollen. Slashed. His body was blotchy with contusions. More than one witness attested to seeing three bullet wounds in his chest (the same number which killed Finn Mullen, in the cemetery, Marshal noted). Tears welled in his eyes but, almost stubbornly, refused to stream down his cheeks. Part of him was tempted to call Grace and ask her to come back, but another part of himself judged that as weakness. Anger was sovereign over grief. The dull ache in his stomach became a pang. Molten lava, rather than blood, coursed through his veins. The former soldier and personal protection officer cursed himself for not insisting on accompanying his friend, until he boarded his plane for Portugal. He thought how, if he had not needed to meet Grace, he would have spent the evening with Foster. Maybe he would now be dead as a result of accompanying his friend. Or, more likely he surmised, Foster might be alive. Marshal poured himself another whisky. He recalled a line from Graham Greene, which a fellow soldier, Michael Devlin, had quoted to him one evening: *"Whisky – the medicine of despair."*

It no longer felt like summer. He no longer felt like shopping for an engagement ring.

Marshal gulped down a bottle of water and popped a breath mint into his mouth. It reminded him of old times – of his routine, before going on a date. Except, instead of now venturing off to a restaurant, Marshal headed towards the local police station.

The reception area was similar – yet different - to a waiting room at a doctor's surgery. The podgy desk sergeant, with half a packet of crisps covering his jumper, asked Marshal to be seated. He added that someone would attend to him momentarily.

A pungent scent of bleach filled his nostrils as Marshal sat down. He considered that the smell was preferable to the various odours the bleach was overpowering. A sullen looking young black man, no older than twenty-one, sat opposite Marshal, tapping away on his phone. His name was Oswald, but he liked to be called "Blade" (he liked to carry a knife and was a fan of the actor Wesley Snipes). The waistband of his tracksuit was sitting halfway down his arse. He was wearing a t-shirt with the word "Gangsta!" emblazoned across his chest. He also wore a cap with the words "Black Lives Matter" on the front, which he had stolen from a pallid sociology student. His beady, bloodshot eyes were as red as a furnace. He gazed at the well-attired Marshal, curling his lip and narrowing his eyes in disdain at the *whitey*, as the drug dealer and petty thief called him in his mind. Marshal, instead of lowering his eyes in submission, smiled in amusement at the youth. He responded by sucking air through his teeth, rather than offering up a bon mot. Marshal fancied that the youth resembled the Somali pirate that Foster had strafed during the attack on the tanker. The drug dealer called his girlfriend again, to hurry her up to collect him. Marshal couldn't quite decipher all he said, but he spat the words of "bitch" and "ting" down the phone more than once.

A busty fifty-something ash-blonde drab, or sex worker, sat in the corner by the door which led into the rest of the station. *Ruby*. Her eyeliner had run, and her tomato ketchup lipstick was smudged. Her skin was puckered, like old leather, and she was wearing only one black heel. The other, broken, was cradled in her lap. Ruby was wearing a red, skin-tight cocktail dress marked with various faded stains. Rolls of fat hung over the edge of the garment. Meth and gin had aged the once attractive, vivacious woman. A couple of front teeth were now missing. Ruby regularly lowered her prices - and was happy to be paid in drugs of late. She considered every man to be a potential customer, so she duly smiled at Marshal, albeit her expression resembled a rictus more than grin.

"Do you like the look of these, luv?" Ruby remarked, cupping her large breasts, sounding like she was auditioning for the part Nancy in Oliver Twist.

"No," Marshal courteously replied. "But thanks for the mammary."

He kept his head down, having little or no interest in the other occupants in the room. Marshal's thoughts were for the dead, not living. It pained him to think of his brutally slain friend, yet Marshal continued to do so. He closed his eyes and recalled some of the things Foster had said the day before:

"I don't want to give the murderous bastard the satisfaction of killing me... I've earned my cowardice and right to retreat from this fight. I don't want to live in London, having to watch my back all the time. I'd rather live in Portugal – and watch the senoritas go by... I want to give you a key to my storage locker. If somehow something happens to me, I want you to remove the contents. You will know what to do."

Marshal's shoes made a comical squeaking sound on the waxed, plastic floor as he was led down the corridor and into a meeting room (as opposed to an interrogation room). Ingots of light slanted through the barred window. The walls were painted a dull beige, the floor a duller grey. Posters marked the walls, warning of the dangers of leaving handbags unattended –

and failing to get one's prostate checked. The menus of half a dozen takeaways were stuck to the door of a small fridge. DI Martin Coulson was waiting for him, a cup of coffee in his hand. The officer was in his late forties and was in good physical condition, having avoided a policeman's paunch. Marshal thought he looked an accountant – or a mid-level civil servant, caught between working for a promotion and waiting for retirement. His cropped black hair was flecked with grey. Intelligent, brown eyes, behind horn-rimmed glasses, could harden or become good-humoured, depending on the circumstances. A cigarette lighter, notepad and half-eaten packet of mints sat on the pinewood table in front of him. He wore an ironed white shirt, charcoal grey clip-on tie and a pair of blue corduroy trousers.

"Sorry to keep you waiting, Mr. Marshal. Can I get you a cup of coffee?" Coulson asked, after introducing himself. His voice was firm but not unfriendly. Marshal fancied that the policeman came from or lived in Kent or Essex.

"No, thank you," Marshal replied.

"I don't blame you," Coulson remarked, wincing a little after taking a sip from the chipped mug. "If this is coffee, I'd prefer tea. But if this is tea, I want coffee."

The detective was attempting to be disarmingly friendly, Marshal thought. But he did not want to be disarmed. For his part Marshal wished to give the impression of still being in shock, or dumbstruck. He liked being underestimated. He gave a vague, polite, forced smile in response to the figure opposite him.

"You have doubtless heard the news. I hope you appreciate that we cannot officially say too much at present. The investigation is ongoing. Rest assured; we are committed to apprehending anyone involved in Mr. Foster's murder. I read his service record before travelling here. He was a good soldier.

I served in the Royal Engineers, more years ago than I care to remember. The army was not for me. My wife complained that I was away from home too much, although I sometimes thought that I was not away enough."

Perhaps, on another day, Marshal might have liked the Special Branch officer. He regretted not doing a bit of due diligence on the officer, before their meeting. Marshal was willing to happily lie to the policeman, however, whether he liked him or not – as he proceeded to reply to the routine questions with routine answers.

"Can you confirm that you had lunch with John Foster at the Albert public house, on Gladstone St, yesterday?"

"Yes," Marshal replied, neither rudely nor courteously, adding the approximate time that they arrived and departed. The timings corroborated those that Coulson's colleague had gleaned from the time stamps on nearby CCTV cameras.

"What was the purpose of your lunch together?"

"Every six months or so we have a catch-up."

"Can you tell me what his mood was like during your time together?"

"His mood was fine. He was fine, from what I could tell."

"Did he say or do anything out of the ordinary to you?"

"No," the interviewee remarked, gently shaking his head, as he clutched the key in his pocket which Foster had passed onto him.

"Did he mention the name John Mullen to you?"

"No," Marshal stated, after pretending to remember. Lying.

"Do you know who John Mullen is?"

"He's an Irish politician, is he not? I apologise. I wish I could be of more help to you."

"I understand," Coulson said, with sympathy, before jotting something down in his pad again. The dogged detective had hoped that the victim's friend could be of greater assistance in their investigation. The ex-Para, who was clearly intelligent, could indeed be innocent, or ignorant, of Foster's past and connection to Mullen – but it was doubtful. The son of a Scottish Presbyterian minister had faith in Man's propensity to lie, both to himself and others. Coulson's Catholic wife considered deception to be Man's original sin too. It was bound up in his DNA, like lust. The policeman had a justly low opinion of people, partly because he had encountered so many over the years. Coulson could not recall an instance over two decades when he had attended court and a defendant had not perjured himself. Coulson did believe, however, that although Marshal may be committing the crime of bearing false witness – he was not involved in his murder. Marshal had an alibi – and no motive. As much as the ex-soldier had blood on his hands from his time in the army and as a PMC, none of the blood was his friend's.

Coulson wanted James Marshal to help incriminate Mullen, not himself. The detective intended to gain as much information as possible, before he interviewed the slippery politician. Coulson and his colleagues would utilise the Terrorism Act to collect what intelligence and evidence they could on Mullen. The Irish statesman would need to be seen to cooperate – and not refuse their request to be informally interviewed – but it was unlikely that their questions would force any answers. His alibi would be even more cast iron than Marshal's. His hands would be as clean as a bride's dress on her wedding day. The encounter would largely prove a waste of time. Yet Coulson was keen to conduct the interview himself. He wanted to look the prospective killer in the eye, hear the timbre of his voice. Know his enemy.

Harvesting potential intelligence was not the only reason why Coulson arranged an interview with Marshal. The detective wanted to, subtly or otherwise, warn the soldier off from interfering with his investigation – to become more of a problem than solution. It was unlikely he would, but the brother-in-arms of the victim owned the means and motivation to confront Mullen, or another suspect, and do more harm than good.

"You will be having a drink or two at the funeral, when you say goodbye to John?"

Jack.

"I imagine I will."

"I would like you to do me a favour - when you meet with John's former colleagues. They will be angry, as well as sad, in response to his death. If you reassure them that we are committed to bringing the perpetrators to justice – and that no one should attempt to take the law into their own hands. You probably know about the old adage that anyone seeking revenge should first dig two graves?" Coulson asked, probingly – forewarningly.

Marshal shrugged his shoulders, nonchalantly, in reply, as though revenge was the last thing on his mind. The innocent expression masked contrary thoughts, however. He gripped the key in his pocket even tighter.

They will need to dig more than two graves once I've finished with them.

7.

Two weeks passed. Two weeks of sleepless nights. Of stinging heat and grief. Two weeks of retreating into himself and feigning interest in what Grace was saying. Two weeks of working his way through ten bottles of whisky. He smoked twice as much as usual. He spent two weeks waiting for someone to start a fight in some of the pubs he holed himself up in. He wanted someone to try and mug him again, so he could explode into action once more, like a blunderbuss. After two weeks Grace stopped coming over. His mood was as black as Erebus. Regret ate into his time and soul, like rust. The only thing which his regret didn't eat into was itself. Marshal reached out to the family of his friend to offer his condolences (and he even offered to cover the funeral expenses, mindful of Foster's preference to be buried). But Foster's first wife tersely asserted how she had already decided to cremate the body. It was the cheaper option.

Most things - even reading and eating - faded into the background. The only thing Marshal could focus on was his research into Foster's murder. The police could neither confirm nor deny any sectarian involvement in the killing. No group claimed responsibility for the murder. A timeline was created for Foster's movements. After leaving Marshal he had travelled across Waterloo Bridge, stopping off at a pub on the Strand. Foster then hailed a black taxi, to take him to the *Cleaver Arms*, ten minutes from his home in Walthamstow. But the former soldier never reached his flat. At some point between the *Cleaver Arms* and his property, he was abducted. The media initially decamped itself on the street where Foster's body was found. They then doorstepped the family and friends of the victim (Marshal was content to ignore any journalist who tried to call or accost him). It was the crime of the year, for a few days. The police arranged more than one press conference. Witnesses were called upon to report on any suspicious persons or vehicles. Marshal noted Coulson sitting on the end of one of the conferences, headed up by senior officers from the Met. His jaw jutted out in grim determination, as he fidgeted with a pen in front of him.

The grisly murder soon became old news, however, as the front pages were replaced by the stories of a popstar changing his pronouns, some mild flooding in Surrey and a Tory politician, who had been an advocate for Brexit, having an affair with a married woman who lived next door to the junior minister. "Love Thy Neighbour," was one of the headlines.

A day before the funeral Marshal decided to finally visit the storage unit which Foster had paid for (using cash, under a false name). The building, which resembled a run-down Ikea warehouse, was situated in Leytonstone. There was little security or due diligence from the staff when Marshal entered. His key served as his identification and authority. The unit was neither the largest nor smallest in the building. It measured the size of a snooker table. The walls were a dirty eggshell white. Cobwebs hung from a naked bulb. Marshal noticed a charcoal grey suit in the corner, covered in cellophane from where it had come back from the dry cleaners, which Foster had worn to his second wedding.

"I only wore it once," Foster had remarked to his friend, gruffly. "Once was one too many times though… She took me to the cleaners in the end."

Marshal suddenly felt hot, observing a large black holdall at the back of the room, and removed his jacket.

He turned his attention to a metal desk, with an accompanying two-drawer cabinet, which ran along one wall. On top were a few pieces of African and Arab sculpture – gifts from satisfied clients from when Foster worked as a PMC. The drawers of the cabinet contained dog-eared copies of invoices, receipts and accounts. He also found a padded brown envelope, filled with a brick of twenty-pound notes. Marshal thought how he would pass the money on to one of the widows, depending on who needed it most. He would lie and say that the sum was an outstanding debt which he owed to his friend. A bag of golf clubs and collection of fishing rods were also propped up against the wall.

Marshal sneezed, from the dust proliferating the room, and felt his phone vibrate in his pocket. It was a message from Grace:

I can still free myself up if you change your mind and want me to attend the funeral tomorrow. xx

Marshal paused, licking a few beads of sweat from his top lip, before replying:

Thanks, but it'll be fine. I'm not sure I'll stay too long.

Marshal did not want Grace to see him too mournful, or vengeful. There was an immediate look of hurt and worry on her face when he originally told her that he would prefer to attend the service alone.

Are you still coming to the book launch tomorrow evening?
Yes.

Marshal had given his word, made a promise, that he would go to the party. He was far from sinless, but the soldier had always tried to be a man of his word, whenever he gave it. He recalled a quote, from *Richard II*:

"Mine honour is my life; both grow in one.
Take honour from me, and my life is done."

Marshal suddenly felt a pang of something – grief, fury or self-loathing – when he realised that he should be making a vow to his friend, to find and slaughter his butchers. Mullen and

Duggan. Anything else would prove ignoble, unjust. He would forever walk around with a stone rattling around in his shoe. He would never know peace, until he went to war with those responsible for his friend's death. Marshal thought that should he pray to God right now, it would be the righteous one of the Old Testament, rather than the forgiving one of the New.

He finally approached and opened the large black holdall. The contents gave him short pause - but did not surprise him. A Glock 21. An old army service revolver. A Browning shotgun. An assortment of smoke and flash grenades. A Smith and Wesson M&P15 Sport II. The dark metal glinted. Black gold. Marshal also recognised Foster's collection of service medals at the bottom of the bag, half-discarded or half-treasured.

I want to give you a key to my storage locker. If somehow something happens to me, I want you to remove the contents. You will know what to do.

Foster's whisky and smoke-soaked words were roughly spoken but clear, like a voice from the grave. Like old Hamlet's ghost, calling upon his son to avenge his death.

His phone vibrated again with a message from Grace, reminding him of the details of the party tomorrow evening. He gazed at his screen saver image, after replying. It was a photo of Grace. Achingly beautiful. She was standing, in a blue and white polka-dot dress, belted at the waist to accentuate her lithe figure. She beamed as much as, if not more than, the summery day around her. When he zoomed in on the photograph, he could see a few wayward strands of blonde hair fall down her clement face. Marshal could also make out the silver cross around her neck, against her smooth skin. The photo had been taken outside of the National Gallery, during one of their first dates. Despite being works of genius, the paintings inside failed to stir his soul as much as her. *Grace Abounding to the Chief of Sinners.* The world really would be a better place if it read more

John Bunyan, Marshal fleetingly thought. As much as he had stared fondly at the image in the past, he now felt it was inappropriate. His brow was corrugated. His soul was in another place. The screen saver should be a picture of Foster or Mullen, to remind him of his grief, guilt and duty. Marshal pressed a few buttons to change his settings, so his home screen remained blank.

8.

Morning.

Light shone through a gauze of blue, marked by wisps of cotton-white cloud.

"It's a nice day for it," more than one person remarked at the funeral, as if it were a wedding. Few people under sixty quite know how to behave at a funeral. Dwelling on one's mortality can prove awkward and distracting at the best of times.

Marshal rocked a little on the balls of his feet, offering up a few courteous smiles and fidgeting with his tie as the mourners congregated outside the chapel. He chatted to a few other attendees. Veterans. He found some of the small talk excruciating, but he nevertheless soldiered on. Marshal had met a handful of the ex-servicemen before, through Foster. There was Frank Chester, a former member of the Black Watch. He bred whippets, served as a school governor at a special needs school and wore a poppy on his lapel all year round. His skin smelled of lavender. Next to him was Nigel Hartnell. Like Foster, Hartnell had fought in both the Parachute Regiment and SAS during the Troubles. Hartnell had once explained to Marshal how he had spent half his time trying to forget, rather than remember, his past. With a mixture of plaintiveness and resentment he confessed how he still suffered nightmares about what he had seen – and what he had done: "I can still sometimes feel the spit on my face, from when the women, widows, used to front up to us during a patrol. When it comes to the Troubles, we bleed on both sides." His breath smelled of rum.

Time can erode the toughest cliff face. Many of the lions had become as frail as lambs, Marshal lamented. Instead of carrying their well-maintained rifle they now clutched walking sticks.

Hairlines and faculties were receding. Tattoos were fading, whilst liver spots grew more pronounced.

The night before the funeral Marshal had dreamed of encountering soldiers who were riled up, with a plan and fire in their bellies to take on Mullen and their friend's killers. He felt relief in the dream, unburdened. Perhaps some of the soldiers would have avenged Foster's death in their prime. But it was doubtful that many could now even remember their prime. Yet, for Marshal, the veterans in front of him provided proof that honour existed in the world. Every one of them was worth ten trade unionists, investment bankers or conceited students with mental health issues caused by climate change. And they were worth, at the very least, thirty virtue-signalling celebrities, who raped or repented on a whim.

Just before everyone started to file into the chapel, Marshal offered his condolences to Cheryl, Foster's second wife – a stewardess turned hairdresser from Chesterfield, who was wearing black leather trousers in a show of grief.

"Jack was very fond of you," she said, half-distracted by her desire to check her make-up once more before the service started.

"And he was very fond of you too," Marshal replied, lying. He remembered how Foster claimed that the wedding had cost a fortune, but it was nothing compared to the expense of the divorce. "The step-kids from the marriage say that they resent me, because I did not spare them the time to get to know me. God knows how much they'd resent me if they did get to know me though."

Marshal sat at the rear of the chapel, his back to the wall, as though he did not entirely trust God. The dull ache in his stomach throbbed, like a bee sting. His mouth screamed out for a cigarette or swig of whisky, but Marshal remained deathly silent. Incense perfumed the sombre air. A bible lay open on a lectern. Candles shimmered along both walls, and upon the altar. Organ music was piped through the sound system, but Marshal neither wanted to hear from or speak to God right now.

An effete vicar, who had never once met Foster, went through the motions, like a bored actor. Haughty rather than holy. Marshal regretted not being more forceful with the first wife in relation to saying a few words during the service and honouring his friend. The widow also chose not to arrange an open casket. Marshal wanted to see Foster once more, to say goodbye to him. The sight of him would fuel his ire too. As the coffin sank into the floor, to the sound of *Brothers in Arms* by Dire Straits, Marshal's heart sank with it.

"And though they did hurt me so bad
In the fear and alarm
You did not desert me
My brothers in arms."

Part of Marshal desired to join the deceased, in heaven or in hell – for life to be over. The former personal protection officer thought again how he should have stayed with his friend – and seen him onto the plane. He also pictured Mullen. The Irish politician had given his own press conference, offering his deepest sympathies to the victim's family. Milking the attention and the chance to play the victim himself. He was being wrongly accused, he argued, like his son had been all those years ago. "History is repeating itself."

Marshal shuffled out, along with the other mourners, and welcomed the breeze on his face. Even some of the most stoical soldiers shed a tear. The two widows clutched each other's hands in mock - or genuine - sympathy. The children appeared solemn - or bemused. Perhaps it was their first funeral. Marshal had lost count of the number of funerals he had attended. Death is a soldier's bedfellow. He withdrew from the throng, desperate for a cigarette. He switched his phone on, having turned it off before the service. Two messages flashed up. The first was from Grace:

Hope you're okay. Love you xx

The second was from Paul, asking him if he wanted to watch the Chelsea game in the bar that evening. Marshal replied to the latter, explaining that he wished he could join him for a drink, but he had to attend a book launch.

Marshal looked up from the phone and observed the figure of Coulson standing at the top of a grassy slope which led towards the cemetery's carpark. He held a large golfing umbrella (although the chance of rain was slim) and puffed out his chest a little. The policeman was standing a post, peering at the crowd of mourners. Marshal fancied that Coulson resembled a shepherd, keeping watch over his flock.

The two men met each other's gaze, without animus or amity. Marshal strolled towards the Special Branch officer. He did not want to appear rude and snub Coulson. He also did not want to give the impression that he had something to hide. They stared at one another from a distance, narrowing their hawkish eyes in scrutiny. They softened their expressions, however, as Marshal reached the crest of the slope.

"I thought I would pay my respects," Coulson said, not mentioning how he was curious to see who might turn up at the service. He wondered if Mullen might send one of his minions to observe the event and report back to his master. The investigator was also not averse to encountering the ex-Para again. He could not quite get a read on the soldier, which was cause for concern enough. The son from a distinguished military family could have gone far in the army - but chose not to. Most Paras Coulson had met over the years considered themselves men apart. Arrogance and aggression were drilled into them - if they did not exhibit those traits already. Coulson was taken back when he came across Marshal's service record in Helmand and beyond. He was no stranger to violence and killing. The Special Branch officer had met a variety of types of killers over the years. Marshal did not fit the normal profile. But that did not mean that he could not be in a class of his own. If anyone could go after Mullen, out of revenge for killing Foster, then Marshal could. Yet surely Coulson was letting his thoughts run away from him. The former soldier had a comfortable life and model girlfriend. His record was clean. No arrests. But that did not mean he was guiltless of any crimes. Yet surely Marshal would have too much to lose, if he decided to take the law into his own hands? Mullen may have been less Catholic than the Pope, but he seemed just as well-guarded.

"Jack would have appreciated the gesture," Marshal replied, forcing the mildest of smiles. A cloud of awkwardness and tension hung in the air, like speech bubbles in a cartoon.

"My father used to say that he liked a good funeral, whatever a good funeral is. Knowing my father, he was probably referring to the good drink-up after the service. We spend half the day remembering the dead – and then the rest of the day drinking to forget. I was hoping to catch you before you had a drink, though, in case you might have remembered anything else. Any small piece of information might prove useful and unlock something larger in the investigation."

"To tell you the truth, I have been trying to distract myself and not dwell on things," Marshal explained, with a slight apologetic look on his face.

A car horn blared in the background, but the two men ignored the noise.

"I understand. I suppose he would want you to get on with your life."

No, he would want me to violently end the lives of the bastards who tortured and killed him.

"And how are you progressing with the investigation?"

"You will appreciate that I cannot comment too much on an unfolding case, but there are a few leads that we are pursuing," Coulson remarked, with clear ambiguity – masking his frustration and disappointment. Coulson had a suspect, but no evidence. The officer had been present when a colleague had interviewed Mullen at his office in Mornington Crescent. His alibi for the afternoon and evening when Foster was abducted and murdered was airtight. Too airtight. His performance was convincing – too convincing – as the former IRA Brigade Commander confessed how there was once a time when he would have wished evil on the British soldier: "I would have even wanted him dead. But there has been too much blood under the bridge. The Troubles are a thing of the past. I buried my son. My baby boy. I also put down my weapons and buried my grievances. I believe in the Good Friday Agreement. My life is now dedicated to peace, not conflict. Words are my weapons. Words of peace and reconciliation. And I must practice what I preach... If I can help in any way, do let me know and keep me abreast of your inquiries. I am as keen to catch the people who did this as much as you, officer." The lines the politicians spouted seemed rehearsed. An air of self-righteousness, as well as self-satisfaction, laced his tone. But no amount of perfume can wholly conceal the smell of excrement. Coulson left the meeting more convinced than ever that Mullen was involved in the murder. But, also, he was more convinced than ever that he would be unable to find sufficient evidence to prosecute the wily politician. There were no forensic traces on the body to work on. No witnesses had come forward to further their investigation. They had failed to identify anyone within Mullen's organisation who would break ranks and provide them with relevant intelligence. Mullen's men were loyal to him, like soldiers to a general. The police – Brits – were the old and constant enemy for the republican. Coulson's investigation was not progressing. Rather it was stuck, like a broken cart in a muddy field. If only he could make some mud stick to Mullen, the policeman thought.

"What about the man you mentioned, the Irish politician? Do you believe that he is connected to the killing?" Marshal asked, deliberating not mentioning Mullen's name, as if it was of little importance to him.

"We have been unable to find any evidence to link him to the murder," Coulson replied, adjusting his collar a little as though it were causing him discomfort.

Marshal noted how the policeman was now wearing a proper, as opposed to clip-on, tie for the funeral. Marshal also noted how the investigator did not entirely answer his question.

"Hopefully, Jack will deliver some justice, when he catches up with the guilty parties in the afterlife," Marshal posited, fingering the key in his pocket to the storage unit.

"I am determined that some form of justice will be delivered earlier than that," Coulson asserted, whilst he cleaned his glasses with his tie. The detective recalled, however, a meeting the day before with his superior. "Sometimes the prey, through luck or judgement, avoids all the traps," the commanding officer remarked, before subtly or not encouraging him to devote greater resources to other outstanding cases.

Marshal could believe that Coulson was determined to arrest any culprits, but determination alone would not be sufficient to apprehend Jack's murderers. Mullen knew the law, as well as the Special Branch officer. Justice sometimes, or often, meant working outside the law.

Coulson's phone vibrated in his pocket. It was a message from his wife, Irene, asking when he would be home for dinner. It was his day off. She had not given her husband the most uxorious of looks that morning when he mentioned he would be travelling into town.

"You need to rest," Irene insisted, pricking his breakfast sausages with more violence than usual. "That job of yours will be the death of you - or me."

Irene nevertheless kissed her husband of more than twenty years goodbye.

"I am afraid I am being summoned home, by the wife. Best not to be on the wrong side of your immediate superior," Coulson said, in good humour. "My daughter is due home from university today and my better half is cooking a special dinner. She will have my head on a plate if I am late."

Coulson smiled as he thought of seeing his daughter, Tessa, once more. He loved her dearly – but despaired that she had chosen to sign-up to Film Studies at university. The degree was less than useless, he would often assert. "It's worth nothing, although it seems it's also worth nine thousand pounds a year in fees!" he routinely complained to anyone who would listen. The policeman was willing to swallow his wife's tolerable cooking this evening, though he would refuse to swallow any "critical race theory" coming out of his daughter's mouth. According to his daughter, he was not "a good feminist" – and his original sin of being a racist derived from him "being white". The freemason and local golf club member just hoped that his daughter would not wear her "I know Foucault about Marxism" coffer-stained t-shirt when they were sat at the dinner table.

"Enjoy your meal," Marshal remarked. Somehow the globules of awkwardness and tension vanished. "My better half has corralled me into attending an event she has arranged for the evening. As much as I am smitten with the host of the party, I doubt if I will be enamoured with her guests."

Left-wing authors. A tautology.

"Thanks. Would you like me to keep you updated with the investigation?" Coulson asked. Was Marshal, like Mullen, an interested party?

"No. You already have enough on your hands, I imagine. If there's a breakthrough I will catch it on the news."

Both men knew that there would be no breakthrough in the investigation. Mullen would have second-guessed police procedures. But he would not have factored in Marshal being part of the equation. It was time to make the call. To Oliver Porter. The dull ache in his stomach subsided, as the ex-soldier thought of the mission ahead.

Blood for blood.

9.

Clumps of chocolate-coloured mud were interspersed with patches of shimmering grass. Barely a cloud scarred the burning blue sky. It looked like it was going to be a fine day, until his phone rang.

Oliver Porter reached into his pocket, moved the poo bag aside, and pulled out the chiming device. The former fixer had been expecting a call from Marshal at some point, but he had not entirely been looking forward to it. Porter suspected that his friend was about to do something honourable or foolish. There was little distinction between the two.

A black and white mongrel, part staffie and part anyone's guess, scampered around him, chasing birds and investigating all manner of scents. Violet sometimes reminded Porter of her previous owner – a friend, widower and former operative, Michael Devlin, who had shot himself a couple of years ago. Porter had inherited the dog, and a quiver of melancholy memories. But, for the most part, Violet was a source of joy and consolation in his life. The reserved ex-Guards officer loved the mutt, more than he would have cared to admit. Dog and owner were taking their midday constitutional. Porter endeavoured to take the route which would allow him to avoid encountering any gossiping neighbours. The financial consultant, as he often described himself, was much admired in the village and considered approachable - he lamented.

Porter was well-attired. He wore a navy-blue *Barbour* summer jacket, russet cords from Jermyn St and a pea-green shirt from *Brooks Brothers*. A wide-brimmed hat, from *James Lock & Co*, a present from his wife Victoria, topped the ensemble off and kept the sun out his eyes. He was similarly well-groomed, having visited *Trumpers* in St James's for a shave and haircut the day before. Porter may have been getting old, but he looked good for his age. Thanks to his wife's encouragement, or nagging, he ate well and took regular exercise. He had cut down his wine and cigar intake. "I am healthier, if unhappier, for it," Porter had half-joked to Marshal, when they had last spoken.

Porter was retired. Retired from attending lunches in *White's* with representatives of monstrous corporations, African dictators, and the British government. Retired from swaying local elections, by bribing or blackmailing candidates from both sides of the House. Porter knew, more than most, how they were all as bad as each other. Retired from arranging passports for fraudsters, criminals and "respectable businessmen" to enter or leave the country at will. Retired from keeping certain stories out of the news to save someone's career - or leaking fake news to ruin someone else's. Retired from introducing smarmy sexual predators to even smarmier reputation managers. Retired from arranging personal protection for vulgar or vicious celebrities. Retired from ensuring that the sons and daughters of Russian oligarchs or Indian industrialists entered the right schools and received the right exam results. If the money was good enough, then so was the client, in the fixer's world. Retired from positing the argument that "Death is the solution to all problems. No man – no problem," as the staunch Conservative would quote Stalin whilst offering certain services. Or he would sometimes mention that "seven grams of lead solves all problems." Porter had employed a handful of ex-soldiers. Often ex-special forces. Killers. The hits could sometimes appear accidental, or others were intentionally bloody, to send out a message. Most of the victims deserved their fate. But not all. Porter was far from proud of some of the things he had done over the years. He had created rather than fixed some problems on occasion. He duly kept his work secret from his wife. He could not forgive himself for some of his misdeeds, so it was unlikely that she would, Porter reasoned. The best he could do was to keep busy and not dwell on past transactions. Porter now filled his days with family time, fishing trips, foie gras, Wagner, Elgar, writing an historical novel set during the Byzantine Empire, collecting (and drinking) vintage port, serving as a school governor, going on holiday with his wife and taking Violet for walks, among other things.

Porter provided Marshal with some work years ago, as a driver and close personal protection operative for an array of clients. He had proved personable and professional. Last year, in exchange for Porter providing his former employee with valuable intelligence on a gang within the Albanian mafia, Marshal had agreed to drive his niece around for a few days, when she returned from New York to settle again in London. Marshal had never been on his payroll for anything but as a glorified chauffeur and bodyguard – but Porter realised how much the ex-Para was a born killer. He had shot the Albanians, without hesitation or regret. Without leaving a trace. The lapsed Catholic had missed his calling, Porter fancied. He was loath to label his friend a sociopath, but Marshal had a switch inside him which he could turn on and off at will. The army had probably polished - rather than forged - the weapon.

Grace had told Victoria about the death of Marshal's close friend. And Victoria had told her husband. Porter called a couple of old contacts, to get a lay of the land concerning the murder. The ex-Guards officer was far from impressed that someone had butchered a fellow soldier and dumped the corpse outside of the Special Forces Club. It was tantamount to leaving a dead priest outside of a church. Special Branch and counter-terrorism officers were confident that Mullen was involved, but the investigation had petered out. The culprits were seemingly ghosts.

It was all but over.

But not for Marshal.

"I thought you might call. How are you, James?" Porter's clipped tone – a product of private schools and parade grounds – was patrician and polite. As a result of Marshal dating his wife's niece, Porter had spent a fair amount of time in Marshal's company over the past year – and considered him a friend. When the two women retired to bed of an evening after a meal, the former officers stayed up to share a dram, inappropriate jokes, and war stories.

"I've been better, and I've been worse. So, same as usual. How are things there?"

"Victoria and the children are finding new and ghastly ways of spending my money. My fellow school governors are sending ever more pointless emails. And the fish seem to be biting in the Kennett for everyone but me. So, same as usual here too."

"I need your help, Oliver," Marshal remarked, neither begging nor demanding. There would not be a need for too much exposition. If any. He judged that Grace would have told Victoria about the killing of his friend. Porter was one of the last half-dozen people in the country who still regularly read the newspapers too. He would have kept abreast of the story. Porter knew of Foster's connection to Marshal. Marshal also judged that Porter would not be surprised if he chose to investigate or pursue Mullen.

"How close were you to him?"

"Close enough."

A brace of crows cawed over Porter's head, perhaps complaining that Violet was disturbing their feeding time. She looked up at the birds and wagged her tail in excitement and friendship. Porter paused, internally sighing. It would be pointless to try and dissuade his friend from his current course of action, even if he explained the carnage it could cause. He would not refuse to help Marshal either. He was damned if he did and damned if he didn't.

"If you email me, in the usual way, and I'll attend to it," Porter remarked, amiably, with a heavy heart.

The two men shared a couple of lines of small talk and hung up. Part of Porter felt like throwing his phone into the field. Let it sink, six feet under. Violet may well mistake it for a toy and fetch the blasted thing, though. One cannot escape one's self, or past, Porter fancied. Marshal was living proof of the assertion. Foster was proof of it also. It seemed that John Mullen had one foot in the past too.

Porter creased his face in pensiveness, as if someone had just told him that an old friend had passed away - or had been diagnosed with cancer. The crow's feet around his eyes became more pronounced, like scars. Before, this morning, his only concern had been to find someone to take care of Violet whilst he went on holiday with his wife. The resort on Reunion was expensive, but not ostentatious. Someone had just let him down, having promised to look after Violet. He would not sleep easy, putting her in a kennel for a week, or even for a day. He would rather cancel the trip. But now Porter had a second thing to fix.

Violet stared up at her owner, quizzically tilting her head to the side a little. She even ceased wagging her tail. Did the dog somehow know that John Mullen had unwittingly declared war on the one-man army of James Marshal?

Smoke poured out of the chimney at the rear of the red-brick chapel. The mourners for John Foster began to disperse. They scattered like ashes, as another funeral party began to congregate in front of the building, white tissues and handkerchiefs visible - like tufts of foam in an ocean of black.

10.

Marshal returned home. Rain began to spit against the window, like a basket of vipers emitting their venom. Coulson had been right to carry an umbrella. Marshal switched on some music, mindful of not playing any songs which would make him think of Grace, and poured himself a large *Talisker*, in honour of his dead friend. He wanted to wash the bitter taste of grief out his mouth. Revenge would taste more fruitful. It had been two weeks. Two weeks of letting Mullen think that he had gotten away with murder. Two weeks of letting Coulson believe that he would not do anything foolish. Two weeks of having Special Branch generate a wealth of intelligence and surveillance, which Mariner could hack and give to him. Two weeks of keeping Grace at a distance, so he would now have space to work in and keep her safe just in case he was compromised. Time had not been a great healer. The wound had not turned into a scar, these past two weeks.

There would be no digital footprint of their transaction. Marshal logged into an email address he shared with Porter and left a message in the draft folder, requesting any and all information on Mullen and the investigation into his friend's abduction, torture and murder. Porter would log-on, read and delete the message. The fixer would then contact Mariner in a secure way, who would put the intelligence together in a dossier for the client. "Money is no object," Marshal insisted.

Porter called his associate a "digital ninja... a cyber Scarlet Pimpernel." Despite having worked with him for several years, Porter knew surprisingly little about his associate. His favourite film was *Sneakers*, starring Robert Redford. He probably still lived with his mother. He often inserted an expletive or two in the same sentence, when referring to Julian Assange. And he displayed more than one symptom of being on the spectrum for autism. But Mariner was reliable and talented, which was all Porter cared about. There were very few systems the former computer programmer could not access. He was a gamekeeper turned poacher. Mariner knew which threads to tug on - which holes were empty, and which contained buried treasure. He regularly hacked the networks of global corporations and foreign governments. Over the past year he had also worked for MI5 and MI6. He helped a counter-terrorist unit trace the funds a Wahabi cell was using back to the Saudi Royal Family. "The infraction will be swept under the carpet, but I imagine we will raise the price of our next arms sale to them by two percent or more, as a form of payback," the hacker explained to Porter. He also discovered an ongoing operation whereby Russian agents were helping to fund trade unions and left-wing activist websites, but his paymasters reacted with amusement rather than anger. Mariner was a digital mercenary on the frontline of the cyber war. It was better to have him pissing inside rather than outside the tent. Whilst working for the security services last year Mariner left a backdoor into the system for himself, so he could bypass firewalls and access government databases at will. Retrieving the information Marshal sought would not be overly difficult or time-consuming.

Sure enough, by the end of the afternoon Porter sent Marshal a message to say he would meet him in London the next day with the relevant information.

A promise is a promise. Marshal could think of a dozen reasons why he wished to avoid attending Grace's book launch event, but he had given his word. He showered and picked out a reasonably ironed shirt. Marshal had no desire to suffer the heat, or Morlocks, of the tube so he booked a cab to take him across London to the bookshop in Chiswick. There are two things certain in life: death and taxis.

The party was in aid of toasting publication for *The Battle of the Bulge: A New History*, by Rupert Ashbeck. Marshal did a bit of due diligence in the taxi and looked up the book and author. Ashbeck was schooled at Stowe and Oxford. After studying PPE, he became a foreign correspondent and reported from various warzones around the world, including Iraq and Afghanistan. Marshal knew only too well how much the Ministry of Defence kept the stringers so far behind the frontline that they may as well be back in Blighty. Ashbeck had been described as "a modern-day William Russell," albeit by his publicist. A couple of reviews had already come out, in advance of publication. One was a five-star glowing review, by Tristram Miller. "Ashbeck writes with sympathy and panache... He is the new Max Hastings. The book is more than a tour de force." Marshal noted how the reviewer had also attended Stowe and Oxford. The second review was less kind, though seemingly more honest: "There is scant that can be considered new about this book, and one only wishes that the author's editor would have reminded Ashbeck that he was commissioned to write a history book about the Battle of the Bulge, not bleat on about current US military incursions at every ill-judged opportunity... The narrative runs out of steam quicker that the Wehrmacht ran out of petrol... Monty would have approved of the author's self-regard and propensity to swap out fact for propaganda."

Marshal's phone vibrated whilst seated in the back of the black cab, with a message from Grace:

Guests are beginning to arrive. So far, I have heard four people bemoan Brexit, two people turn their nose up at the wine, one person tell me their preferred pronouns, and another tell me – twice – how they have donated to Black Lives Matter. Are you on your way? Save me!

The taxi pulled up outside of the bookshop. One window was full of Summer Reading paperbacks, the other housed a pyramid of copies of *The Battle of the Bulge: A New History.* Grace asked the author if he could mention Becky, her assistant who put the window display together, and thank her in his speech. He promised he would - but didn't. As much as Marshal craved at least one cigarette before mustering the energy to endure the event, he went straight in to check on Grace.

There was not a non-white face among the pro-diversity crowd. Guests air-kissed one another. Middle-aged men – journalists who had lost their columns – ogled younger women, hoping that they were at least old enough to remember their by-lines from *The Guardian* ten years ago. The air was riddled with a blend of expensive perfumes. Marshal's eyes watered a little as he moved through the throng clogging up the entrance to the shop. He stood on tiptoe and endeavoured to spy Grace, before finding a quiet corner. Becky thankfully saw him and brought over a glass of wine.

"You look like you could use this," she sweetly remarked. The literature student had a heart-shaped face and bright spirit. She had yet to be besmirched by a callous world. Marshal was a figure of curiosity for her. Grace had told her about his time in the army, but he never mentioned a word about it. Rather he spoke to Becky about Milton, Bernard Malamud, and Alexander Pope. He also seemed to know more about Russian Literature than her uninspiring tutors.

"Looks are not deceiving," Marshal said, taking a mouthful immediately. "Keep them coming. Too much will not be enough. The window display looks great, by the way."

Her face broke into a smile and her spirit burned even brighter as she moved on with the tray of drinks carefully balanced in her hand.

Marshal checked his phone again - just in case there was an update from Porter and some of the files would be available earlier. He then scanned the room once more for Grace, but he still failed to spot her. He did recognise a few faces, however. Phillip Foxton was holding court with a few "fans" in the opposite corner. Foxton had once been lauded as the next Robert Fisk. To boost his credentials the foreign correspondent just needed to find a few more pieces of unexploded Israeli ordnance and be awarded a visiting Professorship at Bristol or Goldsmith's university.

The oleaginous, floppy-haired literary agent, Nigel Raglan, moved around the room – oozing as if he were leaving a trail of slime in his wake. He was a sack of shit in a silk-blend shirt, Marshal fancied - a moth attracted to book sales and young, bare flesh. The ardent socialist was keen to ask people about which accountants they used, to lessen his tax bill, and where he could find a new nanny – "inexpensive but easy on the eye." The self-proclaimed self-made man had been voted Agent of the Year twice, after inheriting the successful agency from his father.

Charles Royce, the "BBC legend," also graced the event with his august presence. The veteran newscaster was talking to a woman, impressed by his namedropping or the size of his pension. Her overly vibrant floral dress nearly activated Marshal's hay fever. Royce occasionally surveyed the crowd, to make sure that people were recognising him. The silver-maned "national treasure" had recently instructed his agent to tell the apparatchiks at the BBC that he would be willing to take part in Strictly Come Dancing, for the right fee. The exposure would provide the necessary leverage for his agent to secure a large advance for his third autobiography. The working title was "Voice of the People". Hopefully, no reviewer would remind readers of his recent comment that he considered the British electorate "moronic and cretinous" for voting for Brexit and Boris Johnson.

Marshal could not be entirely sure, but he thought he saw the literary novelist, Xanda Doleman, through the ever-swelling crowd. Doleman's first novel, *When Evening Comes in Tuscany*, had been a critical and commercial success (Nolan's then wife was able to put the book into the hands of a daytime TV producer, who owned a villa in Tuscany and arranged the programme's Book Club feature). Subsequent novels – *Faulkner's Pillow* and *When Evening Comes Again in Tuscany* – had fallen short of the publisher's expectations, however. Doleman had since changed his agent, twice, but he was struggling to regain the sales and advances of yesteryear. Thankfully, his father had just died, and the only child inherited the family home in Suffolk. He would sell the property to pay-off his re-mortgaged flat in North London. He could not imagine living anywhere else but Hampstead. Rumour had it that Ezra Pound had once lived in the property. Or he sometimes disclosed that Laurence Olivier once lived there, to impress the actresses he knew. Money from the inheritance would help fund his writing, while he changed agents and delivered another book – *When Morning Comes to Tuscany*. To help raise his profile Doleman would approach a contact at *The Independent* and write a piece, declaring that he considered himself non-binary. He had written a similar piece, some years ago, outing himself as being pan-sexual. The author would only support the non-binary community, however, if the paper paid him a pound a word for the article. Doleman was wearing a scarlet cravat and a pained expression, as if to send a message out to the world that no one truly understood him. It was more the case that no one truly liked him.

Marshal shuffled into the corner a little more. He wanted to be out of earshot of Simon Posner, the Conservative MP for one of the safest seats in the country. Posner was as intelligent as David Lammy, as competent as Chris Grayling and as honest as Nicola Sturgeon. In a recent interview Posner had cited Liam Fox as being the politician he most admired. Over the past five years the right honourable member for Maldon had been caught embezzling party funds, selling government contracts to companies he was a board member with, and sexually harassing a colleague in the workplace (Tim, a seventeen-year-old intern). The whip was not removed, lest his father removed his annual donation to the party.

As well as perfume, the air was thick with envy, petty-egos, cronyism, and self-aggrandisement. The chattering classes were chatting too loudly. Cameras were fished out of *Mulberry* handbags and held up, albeit people took more selfies than photos of the event. *All is vanity under the sun.* He overheard Doleman give a sermon on the evils of Brexit. "All Europe is my home," he shrilly protested, unwittingly quoting Oswald Mosley. Marshal felt nauseous, as if staggering around the deck of a listing ship in a storm. Sometimes the world resembled a comedy, sometimes a tragedy. It was tragic because it was so comic – and comic because it was so tragic. If somehow Mullen walked through the door, he would have picked up the letter knife by the till and stabbed him in the throat. He needed some fresh air, or a lungful of cigarette smoke, to right himself.

But then he saw her. Grace. He forgot about the files he was waiting for and what they might contain. He forgot about the contempt he nursed for most of the other people in the bookshop. She was a sight for sore eyes, as welcome as hearing a favourite Christmas song being played over the radio. Her anxious expression softened at spotting Marshal. Grace was the most beautiful woman in the room. She always was – and not just because she had been a successful model. It was more than that. Much more than that. She was the kindest woman in the room, he judged. The most Catholic.

She was wearing a rhubarb and purple full-length pleated dress, belted at the waist, by an independent designer that Grace had championed during her modelling career. Xanda Doleman wondered who she was – and if she knew who he was. He even stopped talking about himself, to take her in. His reptilian eyes lapped her up, crawling over her body like a spider at night. Grace's aspect sparkled like a disco ball. Her almond eyes appeared to lift at the corners, smiling - like her wide, delicious mouth. Her beauty felt bittersweet, however, as Marshal remembered what he needed to do. Duty before love. On any other night he would have made a promise to himself to make love to her. He would have planned how to unfasten the dress whilst planting kisses on different parts of her gleaming figure. But he needed to deny himself. He wanted to unzip the holdall in Foster's storage unit even more. Retrieve the guns. Use them. Tonight was the night when Marshal had to tell Grace that he couldn't make love to her, like a boxer abstaining from sex until the fight was over. They could not go home together. He would tell her that he did not want to see her for an unspecified amount of time. He would ask her to trust her, to have faith in him. He did not want to wholly deceive her. But he knew he could not be completely honest either. He just needed some time away from Grace. Marshal could not be dedicated to killing Mullen, and be a devoted boyfriend. He recalled the quote from *The Quiet American* again:

"Sooner or later, one has to take sides. If one is to remain human."

Grace's heels clacked upon the wooden floor, the sound growing louder as she approached him. His smile was and was not forced as he walked towards her. She laced her fingers in his. He pulled her towards him, unable to tell the difference between silk and her skin. Becky stood to the side, judging it was an inopportune time to serve Marshal another wine. Her lips tasted better than any canape on offer. He breathed in her perfume - sweeter and different to others. The dull ache in his stomach returned, like mild appendicitis.

"I bet you hate everyone here," Grace whispered in his ear, almost kissing it. She had bought a bottle of *Talisker* for him earlier, as well as new lingerie, anticipating that he would come back home with her after the event. If he just wanted to talk about Jack and things, that would be fine too.

"Not everyone, of course. Thanks to that dress, I am still smitten with you. I think I would also only hate them if I got to know them," Marshal playfully replied.

Grace laughed a little, like she used to.

Becky filled his glass. He downed half the measure, wishing it were something stronger. His phone vibrated. He checked to see if it was a message from Porter, but it was just a missed call from Paul. Grace noticed how his screensaver was now blank, as opposed to a picture of her.

"How was the funeral? Did you get to say a few words?"

There was a slight catch in her voice. Her legs felt weak, as if a heel had just snapped.

Her kindness stung him. Burned him. Irritated him.

"No. I'm not sure I have, or can, say goodbye quite yet. Something's still missing," Marshal said, partly to express how he felt and partly to set up his gambit. "I still have some of Jack's correspondence and possessions to go through. I just need some time to myself. I hope you understand."

Grace nodded and replied:

"Of course."

The hurt and discomfort were palpable on her beautiful, brave face. The dull ache in his stomach was replaced by fizzing self-loathing. Grace thought that their time apart would be the beginning of the end. She sensed that there was something Marshal was keeping from her. A pause hung in the air, like a foul smell. The tension increased, like someone turning the screw a couple of times on a garotte chair. Grace's eyes watered, but not from the smell of perfume.

A knife chimed against a wine glass, signalling that someone was about to give a speech. To Marshal, the noise was either a death knell, or a bell marking a break between rounds. The editor, who was now secretly worried that he had overpaid for the book, introduced his author with fulsome, plum-rich praise:

"Xanda has been a pleasure to work with. A gent... The book reads more like a novel than a history book... As much as Europe needs to now save Britain from itself, there was a time when Britain saved Europe... Xanda captures the courage and stultifying fear of individual combatants, the blood and brutality. You can smell the cordite in between the pages..."

As the tittering crowd moved forward, to better hear the speeches, Marshal let go of Grace's hand. Or did she let go of his? His phone vibrated again, this time with a message from Porter, providing details of where and when they should meet tomorrow. The meeting could not come soon enough for Marshal. The money he had saved on buying an engagement ring would be able to pay Mariner's fee, he judged.

Using the distraction of the applause – and Ashbeck starting a speech which, like his book, needed editing – Marshal worked his way through the scrum and went outside, drinking in the fresh air like spring water. His hand trembled as he lit a cigarette, frightened that he had lost Grace. Or he was deliriously happy to be free from the crowd. *Hell is other people.* There was too much phoniness, or civilised society, inside. Too many cutglass accents, spouting insipid or invidious conceits. He had overheard one woman assert that "People from the North should not be allowed to vote, unless they can first prove that they understand the issues at hand." Marshal balled his hand into a fist - but he wanted his fingers to grip themselves around a gun. He hailed a black cab, asking the driver to take him back home. He would send a message to Grace to apologise for leaving early. He did not want to ruin her evening, or life, further.

11.

"As awful as James might feel about the sad death of his friend, he will feel a lot worse if he loses Grace," Victoria had argued, as she drove her husband to the train station.

Porter had nodded, remarking that he would have a word with his friend during their lunch. He said that he was due to meet Marshal in order to provide some financial advice and contacts, in relation to helping him deal with John Foster's estate. Porter might mention Grace in passing, but he did not want to get too involved or meddle. Fixing romantic relationships had never been part of his brief. Porter was also aware that there was method in Marshal's madness. He was putting distance between himself and Grace to protect her. He could not be an attentive boyfriend and concentrate on the task at hand. Porter knew only too well how difficult it was to lead a double life.

The train rocked a little, like a crib. A pleasant vista of verdant fields, hedgerows and a shimmering sky unfurled itself outside the window. He had the carriage to himself, aside from a handful of commuters and an attractive forty-something who sat opposite him. The blonde divorcee, Gloria, eyed him more than once and offered up a suggestive smile. He looked good for his age, she thought. The lawyer noticed his wedding ring, but he seemed wealthy and powerful enough to keep one, or more, mistresses. Porter was wearing a linen suit, with brown brogues from *John Lobb* and a teal shirt from *Harvie & Hudson*. A silver tiepin and silk pocket square finished off the outfit. Gloria was close enough to smell his expensive aftershave – and recognised that his suntan was from a holiday rather than sunbed. A slender, costly laptop – and a hardback book – sat on the table in front of him.

Porter offered up a courteous smile to the lady opposite him, after fastidiously picking a couple of Violet's hairs from his left lapel. She tucked her hair behind her ears, and he noticed how she had freshened up her make-up in the toilet. Porter was familiar with certain indicators of interest. She smiled again and would have said something to her fellow passenger – but he buried his head behind his laptop once more. The fish would not bite. It was the briefest of brief encounters. For all his sins, Porter had remained faithful to his wife over the years, despite ample opportunities to conduct affairs without the risk of getting caught. It was debatable whether he could consider himself a good man, given his previous career, but Porter at least could call himself a good husband and father. Victoria often complained that he had been married to his work, but that was the only mistress he had. He was no angel, but no adulterer too. Porter also fancied that he had remained faithful to his wife because he wanted to prove to himself that he had not turned out like his father, who had constantly hurt his mother when he was a boy, with his barely concealed infidelities.

Porter knitted his brow in worry and disdain as he worked his way through some of the intelligence files which Mariner had sent over. The fixer, who was familiar with statesmen and intelligence operatives who had dealings with Mullen and the IRA, was not shocked by what he read, unfortunately. Mullen initially served as a foot-soldier and recruiter during the Troubles. He had served in the famous, or infamous, Belfast Brigade – the "Dogs of War" as they were known. Mullen had kneecapped Protestants, been involved in the abduction and murder of British soldiers, and been implicated in various bombings, in Northern Ireland and on the mainland. The terrorist turned politician had called himself "the Irish Nelson Mandela" after the Good Friday Agreement had been signed. He had seen the light, "experienced a Damascene moment". It was surely coincidence that his Damascene moment came a couple of days after he was told that his supporters in the US would no longer fund any form of terrorism, in light of the events of 9/11. Mullen not only preached the gospel of the Good Friday Agreement but he laid claim to having the ear of the leading players during negotiations. "More than anyone else, I was the architect of the deal," he claimed in his autobiography, *Green Peace: The Life and Troubles of John Mullen*. "What Northern Ireland needs is good governance, not guns," he preached from the political pulpit, as his lieutenant held an assault rifle to the head of his rivals, to discourage them from running for office against his master. The British intelligence services kept a watch on the person of interest, despite his claims to have "given up the gun". Mullen had not turned his back on his para-military comrades. Far from it. Grainy clips, taken at various backroom and basement gatherings over the years, showed a tub-thumping Mullen still believing in a united Ireland. The "long war" was just that. The phoenix would rise from the flames. Intelligence suggested that Mullen was not just aware of current Real IRA operations, but that he was still issuing orders within the organisation. He was suspected of being behind the recent punishment beating of his brother-in-law, in retribution for an adulterous affair. Mullen was also suspected of receiving campaign contributions from the Real IRA. The freedom fighters were not averse to drug dealing and extortion to fund their sacred cause. Mullen could still be considered a boss of one of the largest criminal enterprises in Europe. Transcripts within the intelligence files also highlighted how Mullen changed his message depending on his audience. In one speech he claimed that a united Ireland should see its future at the heart of Brussels. During another speech, dated a month later, the firebrand statesman argued that a united Ireland should celebrate its independence: "We should not free ourselves from one occupying force, to shackle ourselves to another. Europe is the sick man of Europe! No taxation without representation! We need to take back control!"

Part of the dossier Mariner provided intelligence on covered Mullen's lieutenant, bodyguard and enforcer – Sean Duggan. A weathered, scarred face looked out from the laptop at Porter. Strands of wiry red hair poked out of a broken nose, which appeared as if it had been placed haphazardly on his countenance, like a child pinning the tail on the donkey when drunk. A worn septum betrayed a cocaine habit. Patches of grey mottled the stubble of the ginger hair covering his head and lantern jaw. Duggan's father had been shot by the British Army, during a bout of rioting after Bloody Sunday. He had been just a few years old at the time. Duggan had made his first kill at the age of seventeen. The youth had been a promising boxer and an apprentice plumber, but he put the cause before any personal ambitions. The recruit was given a taste of violence and he thirsted for more. Mullen took the zealous, fearless adolescent under his wing in the eighties. He was the father figure the boy never had. The intelligence report alleged that Duggan served on various killing squads and "disappeared" a number Catholics living on various council estates, suspected of working for the British as informers. Although there was insufficient evidence to force an arrest, Duggan had been the chief suspect in the death of Alice Brady. A single mother to four children, the devout Catholic and nurse had rushed out of her house to attend to a wounded British soldier. For this act of "treachery," Brady was abducted and executed. Her back was flayed, her eyes were gouged out and her breasts were sliced off. After being raped. Mullen, either as a reward for the crime or to take the heat off Duggan, arranged for his lieutenant to travel to Libya. Duggan was trained in counterintelligence and marksmanship. Numerous shootings were attributed to the sniper when he returned to Belfast. Duggan was eventually arrested, for conspiring to commit a terrorist act. Mullen campaigned to have his enforcer released, arguing that Duggan was a victim of being in the wrong place at the wrong time – that he was not terrorist. After the Good Friday Agreement, however, the newly elected politician arranged for Duggan to be put on the list of terrorists who should be released under the terms of the deal.

Although Duggan shared the same alibi as Mullen for the murder of Foster, a Special Branch officer, one DI Coulson, posited that Duggan would have been behind the operation to surveil and snatch the target. Coulson asserted that Duggan's own lieutenant, Fergal Nolan, led the kidnap and killing of the former soldier. Duggan's niece and nephew were also in London just before and after the crime was committed. The pair were known intelligence operatives for the Real IRA. It had also been Duggan's trademark, during the Troubles, to dump the corpses he was responsible for outside their barracks or homes. He had sent the same message, Coulson believed, by discarding Foster's body outside of the Special Forces Club. Again, though, the Special Branch officer's assertions were supposition and circumstantial. Mariner had also included a file from the RUC in the intelligence cache, concerning a spate of sexual assaults committed by Duggan in Belfast. He used his niece and nephew to lure teenage boys and girls back to his apartment. He would proceed to drug and rape them. A case was brought against Duggan – and one of his victims put themselves forward to testify. The youth was found soon afterwards, eviscerated, with his genitals having been stuffed in his mouth. The charges were dropped, and no other victims came forward. Mullen secured various injunction through the courts so Duggan's name was kept out of the press.

Porter scrolled through a few of the photographs of Duggan's victims. The fixer was far from squeamish - but he winced, and his stomach turned, before closing the laptop. Gloria smiled at Porter once more, but he did not have the strength or will to be polite. He thought that Marshal might be biting off more than he could chew. Mullen travelled with security at all times. His properties, an apartment in London and farmhouse outside of Belfast, were well guarded and rife with CCTV. The likes of his car and offices were furnished with bulletproof glass. Porter envisioned the scenario of a captured Marshal being tortured and interrogated. The monster of Sean Duggan could somehow find his way to his own front door. His daughter's bedroom.

Porter's heart and body jolted as the train entered a tunnel - and darkness reigned.

Lunch would be on the terrace at the National Liberal Club. Porter hailed a taxi from outside Paddington Station. He asked to be dropped off at *Farlow's*, where he happily let a sales assistant reel him into buying a new fishing rod and bait box. It was just after midday. Porter allowed himself a pint in *Chequers* on St James's, before buying a few books in *Hatchard's* (David Goodhart's *Head Hand Heart*, Charles Spencer's *The White Ship* and a couple of Eric Ambler novels). Porter bumped into a bookdealer friend in the store, who told him he could get his hands on a first edition of E. W. Hornung's Raffles stories. Porter said he would pay £500 for the book, but not a penny more. He proceeded to pop next door into *Fortnum & Mason's*, where he bought a selection of luxury foodstuffs, by way of an apology to Victoria for cancelling their lunch date. Porter liked buying things, both for himself and others. He wanted something good to come from his less than clean money.

"You are becoming more addicted to shopping than I am," Victoria half-joked the other month. As usual his wife was right. To save himself resembling a well-dressed packhorse, Porter arranged for his purchases to be posted to him.

The club was far from busy, with many of its members away for the holidays. When Porter strolled out onto the terrace, however, he still met someone he knew.

Sir David Peston had been compared, unfairly or not, to Lord Adonis, for his campaigning zeal to re-join the European Union. No personal attack was too spurious, no fact too fictional, no newspaper column too partisan for the Liberal Democrat MP. Physically Peston was no Adonis. Indeed, he looked more like Cyril Smith. Porter quite literally pressed the flesh when he shook his hand. His thick, pink lips were rimmed with red wine. Light reflected off his domed forehead and "Re-join, Rejuvenate" enamel badge. Porter was introduced to Tarquin Thorpe, Peston's lunch guest, who worked as an adviser to aid development officers. His advice was always to spend the budget, lest they try and slash it the following year. Porter did not ask, but Peston proceeded to tell his fellow club member what he was up to:

"I have just been asked to join the *Fair State* think tank. They are even deigning to name an essay prize after me," Peston remarked, placing a palm on his breast, whilst declining to mention that he would only take the position if they named the prize after him. "Gordon and Tony are fighting once more, over me. They would like me to give a speech for their foundations. But they insist that if I attend one, I cannot attend the other. I feel like a young girl, with two date offers for the prom... Did you see me on the BBC? The teaching unions rallied around me immediately... I am still fighting the good fight. We must enlighten the electorate, or ignore it... My flock is growing, as you may have noticed. I now have more fans or followers or what not than Hilary Benn, I am told... I am just a messenger though. The message is more important that just one man... Did you see my piece in *The Observer*? I did it for gratis, or for the cause, of course - but I made the editor pay for it over lunch."

Porter nodded politely, or wearily. He noted how Peston often used religious language in his conversation, as if he were a frustrated vicar. His "flock" referred to his followers on Twitter. He called people who disagreed with him "heretics". A federal Europe was also still "the promised land". Lord Adonis was his "John the Baptist". Porter had a few other choice names for the cretinous peer. Porter dared not disclose his sin to Peston, that he had sided with the "the unbelievers" and voted to leave the EU too.

Porter experienced his own religious moment, as he prayed for Marshal to arrive and save him. Thankfully, his prayers were answered. Perhaps he was not such a sinner after all, Porter fancied.

Traffic hummed beneath them, along the Victoria Embankment. The terrace was bathed in sunshine. The two men greeted one another warmly. Marshal was dressed smartly.

"It's good to see you, James," Porter remarked, his voice as polished as his shoes. He was going to add that Marshal looked well, but he feared it might be interpreted as sarcasm. The burgeoning bags under his eyes betrayed how his friend had been put through the ringer. Or he was putting himself through the ringer. Marshal could also be suffering withdrawal symptoms from Grace. She was good for him. Grace helped the soldier combat boredom and other inner demons. But, in combating Mullen, Marshal would need to unleash the devil in him, Porter mused.

"How are Victoria and the children?"

"Expensive, but worth it, as usual. My daughter has a new boyfriend. His name is Gideon – and that may be the least weird thing about him, I worry. I am tempted to have Mariner run a background check on him, just in case he has a criminal record or, worse, is a member of *Momentum*. I am pleased to say that my son is beginning to appreciate the pleasures of a good single malt. He also appreciates the need to conceal his new habits from his mother. I just need to teach him about Edmund Burke – and some misogynistic jokes – and he will be a man. Victoria is going through a phase of inviting our neighbours around to lunch and dinner. Her plan has worked. To escape further social engagements, I have booked us a holiday."

After having a couple of drinks on the terrace they retreated to the dining area. Porter shifted a little uncomfortably in his chair when he first sat down. When he glanced up, he found himself facing a large portrait of Paddy Ashdown looking down on him. Porter thought how he was not the only member of the public that the enlightened Liberal Democrat looked down upon. Claiming that the sun was in his eyes, Porter moved chairs – and was relieved to find himself staring at Lord Rosebery.

Porter ordered a bottle of Pomerol and some food. Marshal proceeded to talk about Foster, the murder, and his dealings with Martin Coulson. His features occasionally became taut, when he mentioned his friend or Mullen, but his tone remained remarkably even. Emotionless. He was a soldier, debriefing an officer. The fixer listened intently, infrequently interrupting Marshal to ask a question or clarify a point. At one point, Porter realised that he was steepling his fingers, like Sherlock Holmes.

"These files will hopefully make your task easier. But, even if they do make things easier, the job will still be incredibly difficult," Porter warned, as he handed Marshal the USB stick. "To get to Mullen, you will need to take Duggan off the board first, else he will come for you afterwards… Mullen has considerable resources to bear. With just one phone call he can mobilise a couple of dozen foot-soldiers. His security team are paramilitaries. They just dress themselves in suits rather than balaclavas nowadays, albeit not particularly well-tailored suits if the surveillance images are anything to go by."

"It will be difficult for Mullen to speak on the phone, if I blow half his head off," Porter drily countered. "I also know about Duggan. If seven grams of lead solves any problem, I'll need fourteen."

12.

Marshal claimed he needed to meet a friend, so as to cut short the lunch meeting. Not only was he eager to return home and examine the contents of Mariner's files, but he wanted to avoid the subject of Grace. For once the two men did not request the dessert menu or order a brandy or three. Porter was in no mood to be cornered by Peston and one of his tribe, so he paid the bill with his customary fifty-pound tip, left with his guest, and walked towards Whitehall to flag down a taxi. The sky had grown overcast. The air smelled of diesel and damp. Yammering tourists - dressed in all manner of garish garments and carrying selfie-sticks and other paraphernalia - stood in stark contrast to the sombre-suited government employees shuffling from one pointless meeting to the next.

"Let me know how much I owe you for the files – and how you would like me to pay you. I am grateful for your help, Oliver."

"You can owe me a comparable favour, rather than any money. Just make sure you stay alive long enough to pay me back - and promise me something. That if you have any doubts about what you are doing, or if you feel you are unable to complete your mission, you will walk away. Remember that your friend was willing to walk away. There will not be any dishonour in doing the same. We are in Whitehall. Downing St is across the way. This is the home of broken promises. Also, Victoria would kill me if you broke Grace's heart."

"I am not intending to break either Grace's heart or my word," Marshal said, with more conviction than was perhaps warranted.

"If you need anything else, just let me know. Mullen is a problem that I do not help mind coming out of retirement to fix."

"Thanks, hopefully I'll be fine," Marshal replied, as he thought that he could purchase all he would need. He also possessed the contents of Foster's black holdall.

The two friends soon after hailed down cabs and drove off in opposite directions.

Marshal made a pot of coffee when he got home. Whilst he was doing so, he poured the contents of half a bottle of whisky he had down the sink. He wanted a clear head and to be free of temptation. As much as he had drunk as a soldier when he could, he never went out on patrol half-cut or hungover. He checked his phone for any messages from Grace. Nothing. A different kind of ache afflicted his innards. He needed to pour a different kind of temptation down the sink.

Work would save him. Marshal lit a cigarette, downed half a cup of coffee, opened his laptop, and inserted the USB stick. He had already read a wealth of articles on the internet about his target, as well as his self-serving autobiography, but Mariner's files would tell Marshal what Mullen did not want people to know about his past. Politicians were fond of re-writing the past. The brief of his memoir, *Green Peace*, seemed to be to laud and exonerate its subject, whilst denigrating Gerry Adams. The files would allow Marshal to pull back the wizard's curtain. The intelligence was extensive, going back decades. They also covered the recent surveillance operation and investigation into the murder suspect.

The Mullen clan might have been considered republican royalty. The history of the cause ran through the family, like words running through a stick of rock. John Mullen was always heir apparent to be a Brigade Commander – or rise even higher.

Intelligence reports recorded that Mullen had taken part in punishment beatings, extortion and robberies as a teenager. Mullen was a gangster as much as a terrorist. It was not long before he also took part in "floats" where, along with a few other armed volunteers, Mullens would ride around the streets of Belfast in the hope of encountering and firing upon a British Army patrol. During his time in the Belfast Brigade Mullen was a participant in torture sessions, executions and bombings. One of his signature torture techniques was to use a razor to remove a victim's skin and flesh, so they could glimpse their own shin bone. His pipe and nail bombs killed soldiers and civilians alike. Nothing could quite be proven for certain, however, then or now.

Mullen's reputation, authority and responsibilities grew within the Provisional IRA, both on the political and military front. He wrote various pieces of propaganda, condemning the faction within their ranks which advocated Marxism – and Ireland becoming a socialist state. "The IRA should not endeavour to be the ANC. I have no intention of spilling my blood to free myself from British imperialism, to then live under the yoke of the Soviet Empire. I am a Catholic, not a comrade."

Some of the intelligence could have been classified as hearsay. The author of *Green Peace* was a far from disinterested commentator. Mullen claimed to have a hand in designing the logo of the Provisional IRA, in the form of a phoenix rising from the ashes. He argued that he was instrumental in securing funds and arms from the Libyans when the IRA negotiated with Colonel Gaddafi. Similarly, it was his decision for the IRA to adopt the Armalite rifle as its weapon of choice, to improve the firepower of their soldiers and become a force to be reckoned with.

What was tellingly absent from the "tell-all" autobiography, as opposed to being covered by the intelligence files, was

Mullen's involvement in rooting out informers in the organisation. Not all loyalists could have been described as such during the Troubles. The British, through bribery or other forms of coercion, compelled a surprising number of volunteers to betray the cause. The punishment for informing was a single bullet to the head. The files alleged that Mullen was responsible for pulling the trigger on over a dozen of those bullets, until he charged Duggan with finding and punishing touts on the Divis housing estate, and elsewhere.

Duggan embraced his new duties, arguably displaying too much zeal. The thug was judge, jury and executioner in some instances. The killings were not always sanctioned by the Army Council or Brigade Commanders. Duggan abducted combatants and non-combatants alike. Before firing the ritual bullet to the head, Mullen's lieutenant would interrogate/torture his victims. Chip fat was poured over the head of suspected touts. Genitals were burned or cut off with butcher knives or garden shears. Eyes were gouged out and stuffed into mouths. Kneecaps were drilled into. One intelligence report speculated that Mullen used his position – and Duggan – as a tool to remove rivals and enemies within the Provisional IRA. As well as battling with other paramilitary organisations, there was endless in-fighting between factions within the command structure. For some, the bombings were too frequent or not frequent enough. Victory could only come via militaristic – or political – progress. Gerry Adams and the Northern Command had too much, or not enough, power. There were too many, or too few, attacks on the mainland. Marshal read one aside in a report about the various nicknames and codenames they gave to the opposing, squabbling groups.

The Big and Little Enders. The Capulets and Montagues. Liverpool and Everton.

As well as reporting on a rise of people being disappeared, Marshal also scrutinised a file which speculated on Duggan being behind an increase in sniping in Belfast, after he returned from his training in Libya. A couple of Mullen's rivals were assassinated. One killing involved a member of the Belfast Brigade, Tommy Byrne, being assassinated outside an office that Mullen occupied in the city centre. The shooter had positioned himself on the roof opposite the offices. Byrne was due to have a meeting with Mullen. In theory, it was an ambush rather than an assassination. Duggan had cut down his target with just one shot. It was a shot that most snipers would be proud of. Marshal mused that if ever he entered into Duggan's sights, it wouldn't be for long.

Marshal read on. The self-proclaimed "man of peace" still ordered punishment beatings during the Good Friday talks. It was difficult to tell how much the likes of Adams, McGuiness and envoys in the British government excluded Mullen from the high-level discussions, or how much he initially stood apart, lest the wind changed and he was considered a traitor to the cause. Although it was debatable how much credit could be given to Mullen for the Good Friday Agreement, he certainly profited from it. He won a seat in parliament, through dubious campaign methods. The soldier re-branded himself as a statesman. Speaking tours ensued in the US. He popped up as a regular commentator on various news outlets. Intelligence reports cited how Mullen still remained close to the Real IRA. The US speaking tour served as a front for Mullen to fund raise, although after 9-11 the well ran dry in relation to donors electing to finance terrorism. America's sudden but understandable reluctance to put money into the coffers of those who utilised violence and terror was one of the principal reasons why the IRA sued for peace. *The sinews of war are infinite money*, Marshal thought, quoting Cicero.

John Mullen was adept at covering his tracks. He regularly used burner or encrypted phones. Criminal and terrorist activities were carried out by proxies, like Duggan. He could always claim plausible deniability. His money was laundered by the same accounting company which serviced Russian oligarchs. There was neither a paper nor blood trail to his misdeeds. The authorities could never quite find enough evidence, or witnesses willing to testify against Mullen. The politician secured elements of diplomatic status for himself and key personnel too, which meant that even if charges could be brought against Mullen, he may still be immune from prosecution. Although Coulson was able to deploy watchers to surveil his suspect, the powers that be refused to allow his team to bug the politician's home and office. The Special Branch officer was fighting with one arm behind his back.

Marshal read the surveillance reports intently, although the operation yielded little valuable intelligence to help build a case against their target. But Marshal was not looking to build a case and operate within the law. It seemed that Mullen did not just deceive his constituents on a regular basis. Not only did he lead a second life, in relation to his ties to the Real IRA, but few knew about his mistress, one Josephine Quinn. It was unlikely that the love nest Mullen had set up for the ex-escort possessed bullet-proof windows. The surveillance report also revealed that Mullen rarely travelled unaccompanied. Duggan stuck to him like a barnacle. He upped the security detail after the murder, as a precautionary measure. Mullen's driver also carried a gun. His apartment building and offices contained CCTV. Planting an IED was out of the question, for fear of injuring others. The politician, due to various commitments, amorous or otherwise, did not appear to have a rigid schedule from week to week. It would be difficult, but not impossible, to plan something in advance, Marshal surmised.

As well as files on Mullen and Duggan, Marshal took particular note of the material on Fergal Nolan. Coulson had not questioned the auxiliary member of Mullen's security team, although Duggan had provided the policeman with alibis for his colleagues. Their statements unsurprisingly corroborated one another's. Coulson noted that Nolan had travelled to Cuba a couple of days after the crime. Nolan had flown back to London, via Belfast, in the past week, however.

Marshal took in a few photos of the thirty-year-old suspect. He looked like a young Paul Gascoigne – but dour, with short ginger-hair and a torso covered in tattoos of IRA and Celtic FC emblems. Most of the photographs consisted of Nolan dressed in an array of tracksuits, topped off with a baseball cap, talking to fellow persons of interest to the RUC. It seemed that Nolan spent half his time in the gym, and half his time in various pubs. His build was compact, muscular. Cauliflower ears betrayed how Nolan had followed in the footsteps of his cousin, in more ways than one, and boxed.

Far more than a united Ireland, Fergal Nolan was motivated by the causes of greed and power. He was an ambitious drug dealer and gangster in his own right, as well as occasional enforcer for Mullen. Nolan had experienced the occupational hazard, twice, of serving time in prison (he refused the offer of a commuted sentence in exchange for informing on his confederates). The first time was for GBH, the second for possession of drugs with intent to supply. Other suspected misdeeds included armed robbery, extortion, bribery of a public official. There was a list of other various violent crimes Nolan was connected to. He was alleged to have stabbed a member of a rival drug gang in a pool hall, with a broken snooker cue. During his youth, Nolan worked as a debt collector. His signature, when torturing one of his victims, was to slice open a captive's nostrils and septum with garden secateurs. Police reports also cited that Nolan had regularly tortured people using a clawhammer, pliers and craft knife. He utilised the latter on a rival loan shark, attempting to move into his territory, by cutting off his eyelids, before dumping his body in acid. He had also been known to squirt lighter fluid over his victims and burn people alive.

Marshal read on. More evidence of an unpleasant worldfilled with unpleasant people. Grace had once argued than the was as much light as there was dark in the world. Marshal said that he wasn't so sure. Or he was sure. There was so much more darkness than light. He proposed that it was almost a mathematical equation: "There are more cardinal sins than cardinal virtues. But that's not the only reason why the tally will always number more for the former than latter."

13.

Oliver Porter made himself scarce and retreated to his glorified shed. He would tie some flies, read, and maybe nap with Violet sleeping by his feet. He explained to his wife beforehand that she might want to spend the evening with her niece without him getting in the way. "I'd feel like a fifth wheel." Porter was keen on being absent when the conversation inevitably turned to the topic of Marshal. He was in no mood to get drawn into either condemning or excusing his recent behaviour. His wife already sensed that something was amiss with the ex-soldier - or Grace had told her something was amiss.

"How was James today?" Victoria asked, *almost* nonchalantly, when he returned home.

"A little pre-occupied. I think his friend dying in such a brutal manner has affected him. I would advise Grace to be patient with him."

"Are you sure that's all it is?" she suggested, less nonchalantly, narrowing her eyes, as if she were the member of a jury, scrutinizing a witness.

"I can't be sure, of course. I do not have a window into my own soul, let alone anyone else's," Porter replied, more humorously than defensively. Just because Marshal and Grace were at odds with one another, that did not mean that he should have a falling out with his wife as a consequence.

"I just do not want Grace to get hurt."

"He will be hurting himself if he does. I recommend we give him some space. Absence will make the heart grow fonder. It's a maxim I am willing to test this evening, by leaving you and Grace alone to talk. I will fetch a couple of good bottles of wine from the cellar for you," Porter remarked. He realised that if he chose the wine then his wife could avoid, accidentally or not, removing the best bottles from his beloved cellar.

"I would recommend to James that he does not give Grace too much space. You do know that she wants to marry him?"

She may well become a widow, before she becomes a wife.

Mullen sat behind his desk, with his itinerary for the following day in front of him. His secretary, Caitlin, had briefly discussed it with him and left. He had pursed his lips as she walked out the office. The priapic statesman liked his female staff to wear skirts. The shorter the better. Caitlin was dressed a trouser suit, again. Her new, severe, haircut did little for her too. She was beginning to look like a lesbian, or a Labour councillor. Mullen had conducted an affair with his assistant over a decade ago, when she was under forty. Caitlin had conducted herself with discretion and professionalism during and after the fling. When his roving eye inevitably turned to metal more attractive, she was sensible enough to not cause a scene, lest he terminate her contract, or have Duggan punish any disloyalty or ingratitude. As much as he told himself that Josephine had made him a one-woman man, it was time perhaps to employ some fresh meat, Mullen thought. It was time to give another young Irish girl a leg-up. He was wary of forcing Caitlin to retire, though. She was loyal and efficient, after all. She also knew too many secrets. Mullen noticed how the secretary had pursed her lips when mentioning his dinner tomorrow night with Josephine. Older women hate younger ones as much as Catholics hate Protestants, he judged. A compromise would be to re-define her duties, so she worked in one of the back offices. She could wear as many trouser suits as she wanted there.

He glanced down at the typed-up itinerary in front of him. He was being taken out to dinner by a group of green energy lobbyists that night so he would get in late tomorrow morning.

He had a few calls to make once he got to the office. One was to an unofficial business associate, back in Belfast. They would discuss buying a workspace above a fast-food outlet. The stench of fried chicken they pumped out would conceal the smell of weed they would store and distribute from upstairs. He had to take another call with one of the producers of *Question Time*, to discuss another appearance on the show. He liked it when Mullen attacked the Tory on the panel. "You piled in on him in the studio, and then there was a pile-on from a twitter mob," the former *Independent* journalist had said to him, gleefully. "I am a soldier on the frontline of the culture war," the one-time student union rep had boastfully remarked to Mullen, adding that he believed in a united Ireland. The Irishman felt little solidarity with the tee-total champagne socialist, however. He wasn't involved in any war that the republican recognised. And he certainly refused to call him "a soldier". Late afternoon would be spent giving a speech at the offices of the charity *Freedernity*, a poor man's *Amnesty International*. The organisation was not so poor that it could not afford a Mullen fee, or an army of chuggers.

As well as having dinner with Josephine tomorrow evening, Mullen was keen to see her tonight as well. She would want him to come to her apartment, no doubt, but he would insist that she come to his place. She would say she needed money for a black cab yet book an Uber and pocket the difference. Mullen had known mercenaries who were less mercenary. It had proved cheaper when he just paid for sex. But she was worth it. Josephine made him feel young, virile. The lauded statesman smoothed his hair across his head, so as little of his bare scalp showed beneath his thinning hair. He pursed his lips again. The packet of Viagra had just one pill remaining.

Duggan tapped away on his phone, slumped upon the sofa, as he confirmed the staff rotas with some of his team. The Head of

Security took another swig from his ice-cold bottle of beer. Beads of sweat ran down its neck. It was time to relax. His gun and shoulder holster lay on the table. Duggan looked forward to an evening off. He slid his hand inside his pocket and touched the bag of coke once more. He might book an escort or watch over the video again of the Brit being tortured and killed.

"It was the bastard's funeral yesterday. Is everything else dead and buried too?"

Mullen was confident that he was in the clear, but every few days he asked his lieutenant for an update. The statesman had a lot to lose if he became complacent. Twice a day he would have Duggan sweep for any surveillance devices.

"The investigation is still active, but they are chasing their tails. They've got something between nothing and sweet fuck all, boss. As much as a few of the bastards may suspect you're involved, they cannot prove anything. I've been told that Coulson has a particular hard-on for you, but he can't keep it up forever. Nolan cleaned the scene. Even if they somehow get to Nolan, they will still be empty-handed. What's the worse that they can do at an interrogation session nowadays – serve you a lukewarm tea or stale biscuit? The fuckers have got more chance of finding Lord Lucan than making our boy talk."

"I almost wish that the likes of Coulson had something on me, so they would bring me in. With the money I could get from suing them for wrongful arrest I might be able to afford to divorce Mary," Mullen said, half joking, as he poured himself a whiskey. "Give Nolan a bonus, to keep him sweet. He's a good lad. An asset."

"Aye, he knows when to open his mouth and when to keep it shut. He's willing to learn, and he's willing to teach," Duggan replied, with a measure of paternal pride in relation to his second-cousin. "I was talking to Danny O'Connor yesterday. He says that some of the old boys were toasting you in the pub the other day, celebrating that you finally got your man. I told them that it wouldn't be the last shot fired in the war. Rather, it'll be the first of many."

"Our day will come," Mullen said, quoting the IRA motto, holding up his glass to his companion. "You should treat your niece and nephew too, for their work. Buy them a keg of Guinness. On me."

Duggan nodded, although he thought how his niece and nephew would prefer some weed or a new games console as a thank you.

"Even fashion models can suffer from pride and vanity it seems," Grace joked, forcing a smile, as she sat around the kitchen table with her aunt. They were working their way through their second bottle of wine. "I said to James that I am here for him, but how many times should I say that before I bore him and myself? I can't listen if he doesn't want to talk."

Grace tucked an errant lock of blonde hair behind her ear, smoothed out her dress and straightened a ring on her finger, so the sapphire faced upwards, but there was a sense that things were fraying in her body and soul, Victoria felt.

She was close to crying. The forced smiles grew even more unconvincing. The measures of wine grew larger. Grace glanced through the window. The fragrances of the nearby rosebushes and freshly mown grass wafted into the kitchen. A clear sky revealed a vista of stars, in cruel contrast to her gloomy mood. She had hoped that Marshal would come back to her house after the launch party. She would make dinner. They would make love. The funeral was over, signalling an end to the chapter, Grace believed – or wanted to believe. Yet she feared that Marshal was becoming even more withdrawn. He was a ship, about to sail over the horizon or off the edge of the world. It was entirely plausible that she might never see him again.

Grace felt as mournful as a widow. Victoria subtly, or unsubtly, hinted that she would be able to find someone who would like her in the future. But Grace was doubtful whether she would find someone who she liked, or loved, more than Marshal.

She had prayed for him, more than once, over the past fortnight – even visiting a local chapel to do so. Sometimes Grace felt guilty, praying for Marshal to come back to her for selfish reasons. She would be willing to downsize and give up her house if it meant moving in with him. Grace also realised that she was feeling something akin to grief. It was not that she was losing him. It was that she had lost him already and was experiencing the various stages of grief: denial, anger, bargaining, depression. She was not quite willing to admit acceptance. Yet.

Grace was sure that there was no one else - Marshal was not having an affair - but that brought little consolation. It meant that she might be the cause of the problem, or their relationship had run its course. There were too many threads that her mind could pull upon and cause her mood to fray even more. Marshal was not the only one to suffer sleepless nights.

"James is not stupid. Oliver said that he just probably needs a bit of time and space. Everything will be okay," Victoria said, as convincing as one of Grace's smiles. "It's the price of being with a soldier. We know them enough to know that they will always keep part of themselves hidden. They go dark. And they believe they are doing so for our protection. I have seen the thousand-yard stare on Oliver. You have probably seen a similar haunted expression on James, when he thinks no one is looking. It seems like he is glaring into nothingness, or the past or future. We will never know. Nor do they, I imagine. It's a sorrow with reason. But you should cultivate a faith, with or without reason, that will help you combat what you might be feeling. James will come back to you. If he doesn't, it's his loss."

Victoria placed a comforting hand on her niece's arm, but Grace barely felt a thing. Marshal was similar to Schrödinger's Cat. Her relationship was both alive and dead at the same time.

"Thanks. I needed tonight. I have been spending far too much time alone in that big house. How did you get to be so wise?" Grace warmly remarked, feeling a little better - albeit she could not feel any worse.

"It must be wine talking," Victoria replied, as she topped up their glasses.

The bedroom was richly furnished. Most purchases he had put on his expense account. The décor was a mix of the old and the new. His mistress had been responsible for the new. A narrow, half-filled bookcase stood by the door. A specially commissioned painting, depicting the Kilmichael Ambush, hung opposite the bed. Mullen had installed a safe behind the picture, containing cash and an additional passport, in case he ever had to leave the country in a hurry.

Josephine first slumped upon his flabby torso, breathless, and then rolled off him, having pretended to orgasm at the same time as Mullen. Her breasts heaved up and down, still glistening with massage oil. She had come over from Cork, in her early twenties, with the intention of following in the footsteps of her mother and being a nurse, but London was expensive. The streets are paved with gold for those who are already rich. At first Josephine spent time web-camming to pay for her studies. Several of her "fans" said she looked like one of *The Coors* – but with augmented breasts. A friend then introduced her to escorting: "You can earn more in one evening that you do now in a month... Just lie back and think of Michael Kors handbags... You will have most clients by the balls, quite literally." After some initial nerves and awkwardness Josephine embraced her new profession. She enjoyed playing a part and making her clients feel special. Sex for some men worked better than prescription drugs for curing boredom or depression. Her nurse's uniform was finally of some use. Josephine, or "Beauty" as she sometimes called herself, worked her way onto the party circuit and slept with a procession of actors, footballers, and politicians. She suffered some bad experiences, but not enough to compel her to stop. Eventually, Josephine had to choose between her studies and her job, which afforded her a standard of living that nursing would never be able to compete with. The high-class independent escort secured a handful of regular, affluent clients. English was her first language. She could hold her drink and a conversation. She seldom put in a bad performance, in or out of bed. She worked hard to maintain an enviable lifestyle. Josephine was also mindful of sending money back home to her family, so her younger brother could afford to attend university. She explained to her mother that she secured a position of being a carer for a couple of wealthy, private clients. She bought an apartment in Battersea, dined out regularly, wore expensive clothes and travelled extensively, both with clients and a couple of other escort friends. Her experiences as a trainee nurse gave her an aversion to drugs, so her body and finances were in good shape. Although it can seemingly be teased out, time waits for no woman. Josephine decided to retire and become Mullen's full-time mistress. The politician treated her well, knowing full well that if he didn't then she could easily find a different patron to keep her in the kind of style she had grown accustomed to.

Josephine had wanted to give herself - as well as her older lover - a good workout, having not attended the gym. Strands of jet-black hair clung to her sculptured, sweat-glazed face like slithers of spinach sticking to a dinner plate. She grinned, hoping to make Mullen grin too – to help convince him of the good time he was having. Josephine, as was her habit, also stroked the white hairs on his chest and hooked her leg around his. She decided she would stay the night. His apartment was close to a favoured nail bar, which she would visit in the morning. She would also make love to him in the morning and, afterwards, ask him for some money to buy a new dress for their dinner that evening. He would be too tired and enamoured to refuse her, she judged. Mullen often said that he "wanted her" in his messages, but never that he "loved her" – which, for the courtesan, was preferable. He liked to be dominant with her, a slave to her submissive role playing. Mullen had recently spoken a couple of times about divorcing his wife, but Josephine had no ambition to marry her client. She enjoyed her freedom and life of leisure and luxury too much. He would make her sign a pre-nup, and ultimately secure a new mistress once she became his wife, who might cast a spell over her husband like she had done. Josephine had not wholly given up hope of finding someone special and marrying for love, as well as money. She also wanted a dog and a child – in that order. The former escort still saw a couple of old clients – a CEO of a hedge fund and a disc jockey. Should Mullen return to Belfast soon, she would accept the CEO's invitation to travel with him to Zurich on a business trip.

Mullen sighed heavily - or wheezed – his old dugs moving a little, like blancmange on a plate. Satiated. Once he regained his breath, he would smoke a cigarette. He welcomed the breeze from the oscillating fan in the corner. Duggan had instructed him to keep his windows closed after the killing of his enemy, just in case. He felt good, although not quite as good as when he had consummated his revenge. The father had finally honoured his son and kept his promise to himself, made all those years ago. He had the name, and he had finally obtained justice. Toynbee's book (the Corbynite had sent him an advanced, signed copy) had lit the touch paper. Although his wife might guess that he was behind the murder, he would refrain from confessing to her. Ideally, she would soon be his ex-wife. It was best to keep her in the dark, about various aspects of his life.

"I don't know whether you will be the death of me or make my life worth living," Mullen charmingly, if still a little breathlessly, remarked to Josephine, placing his podgy fingers on her taut thigh. His wedding ring was cold on her skin, but she barely noticed it.

"You're a better lover than men half your age," the courtesan replied, rubbing her leg against his.

"Flattery will get you everywhere, lass."

She grinned and giggled, coquettishly.

"You seem less tense tonight. But you have raised a smile, as well as raised other things, more this evening."

"You know me too well," Mullen said, not knowing if this was a good thing or not, squeezing her thigh, affectionately, as best he could. "I have had things on my mind these past couple of weeks. But a burden has been lifted. It's now a dead issue."

Mullen closed his eyes and pictured the look of terror and agony on Foster's face as Nolan tortured him. Or rather Nolan was just a tool. "The Big Man" had ultimately tortured and killed John Foster. The soldier turned statesman gently grinned too as he heard his victim's screams, from the video, over the sound of the whirring fan. The noise was as welcome as a hymn from any choir.

The day when he had assassinated Byrne had felt good. But the night when he had heard news of the death of Foster had felt even better, like he had atoned for his sins. Finally, he might find some peace.

Music played in the background. Dylan, again.
"Got nothing for you, I had nothing before
Don't even have anything for myself anymore."

Marshal finally closed the laptop, squinting and pinching the bridge of his nose. He had just emailed Porter, asking if he could contact Mariner for some information. A plan was forming – falling into place like the squares on a Rubik's cube.

The dead of night. Air pollution extinguished the starless sky, like a blanket being pulled over a corpse. Marshal heard a woman laughing from the street outside, drunk or happy. One can equate to the other. The sound spiralled up through his open window and caused a pang in his chest. He regretted having poured the whisky down the sink. It was too late to call Grace or send her a message. Sometimes she woke up early and would read or go for a run, but not this early. Marshal decided that he would not get in touch even when she stirred though. He needed to be on point. He would soon begin to stalk his prey, with an eye to snaring it. Just over or under half of him wanted to hear Grace's voice. See her. Kiss her. But Marshal needed to deny himself. Punish himself, for past and future sins. As a Catholic, Grace might appreciate his abnegation. But she would never know.

Her perfume was fading in the apartment, being replaced by the scent of gun oil. And cigarette smoke. His breath must reek, Marshal thought. Thankfully, or not, he would not be kissing anyone goodnight. The ashtray was overflowing. The pyramid of butts appeared as if it might collapse under its own weight at any moment.

Marshal heard another burst of laughter from outside and felt another twinge. The dull ache in his stomach was now different. Making Grace laugh was one of his favourite things in the world. It never got old. He noticed how a layer of dust was forming on his books and furniture. Only now did he begin to appreciate how much Grace kept his home clean and tidy. The day they spent in the chapel, where he prayed and thought about marrying her, seemed an age away. He felt as weary as a medieval pilgrim who had just learned that Jerusalem was no longer in Christian hands. Life had whittled away at him. Life was not sculpturing him, to turn him into something beautiful, useful or good. Life was just eroding him, turning him into nothingness. Grinding him into dust.

"The emptiness is endless, cold as clay,

You can always come back, but you can't come back all the way.

Only one thing that I did wrong
I stayed in Mississippi a day too long."

14.

His head was throbbing like it was the morning after. But the night was just beginning for Fergal Nolan, unfortunately for him. The last thing he remembered was walking home and blacking out, but not from the five pints of Guinness he had consumed in one of his local pubs in Kilburn. His crown hurt, but again not from the Guinness. Marshal had appeared out the shadows on a quiet side street and struck his quarry on his head with a cosh. He had waited there the previous two evenings for Nolan to walk past on his own, but the street had been occupied with passers-by. But the soldier was used to being patient. Marshal quickly bundled the brutish rag-doll body into the back of a large white van he had rented for cash, under a false name. He secured his prisoner and injected him with a mild sedative, to keep him quiet while he drove to the location in Kent which Mariner had provided. No one looked twice at a white van in Kent.

A week had passed since Marshal first pored over the intelligence files. He focused his reconnaissance on Nolan, heading out each day with a bottle of mineral water and a copy of Graham Greene's *The Tenth Man*. The thug would be the key to unlocking the door to get to Duggan and Mullen. The locations of both pubs that his target frequented meant that Nolan would pass through an alley, leading onto the street where he lived. There was an absence of CCTV cameras in the area. Marshal's pulse raced, with gratification as well as nerves, when Nolan had walked through the alley, coughing and then spitting out some phlegm.

Although initially groggy and disorientated, Nolan soon took in his surroundings and the dire situation he was in. The van was a similar size to the one they had used to kidnap the British soldier. Tall enough for a man to stand up in. Nolan's face was pale – and not because he was Irish. The air was still balmy, yet the captive understandably shivered. His shoes and socks had been removed. The back of the vehicle smelled of a mixture of oil, bleach, and fried chicken. The worn, dark carpet resembled burnt toast. A solitary, dirty, cobweb-strewn bulb hung down from the roof. The prisoner was strapped to a metal chair, back, arms and legs. He hummed and grunted through the tape covering his mouth. Plastic ties cut into his wrists, fastened behind his back. The more he struggled, like a worm wriggling on a hook, the more they bit into his skin. But still he struggled, in vain.

Nolan was accustomed to being the abductor, rather than abductee. The enforcer was always mindful that he could one day receive a taste of his own medicine, but he believed he would be in danger in Belfast, not London. His mind raced as best it could, tripping over hurdles, as Nolan thought who could be responsible for his present fate. He had plenty of enemies, but few would dare to make such a move. If he got out of this alive, the relevant enemies would be dead men walking, he vowed.

Marshal, having stationed himself behind his captive, appeared in front of Nolan, after noticing him stir. He was wearing a black balaclava, along with a black t-shirt, black jeans, black, steel capped boots, and blue surgical gloves. Nolan's bulging eyes were wide with rage or terror, as if they were about to burst out of his head like a cartoon character. He checked out Marshal's forearms for any revealing tattoos, but there were none. As menacing as it may have been to see the figure towering over him, wearing a balaclava, Nolan took comfort that his enemy was keeping his face hidden. If he showed his face, then it was likely Nolan would be killed to prevent him from taking his revenge or identifying him. He was pleased to see a lack of plastic sheeting on the floor too. There was a good chance he could survive the night.

"I am going to torture you, like you tortured John Foster. But, unlike John Foster, you will have the opportunity to come out of this alive," Marshal remarked, his voice as calm as a rockpool. He was unerringly courteous, before potentially being unerringly cruel. Marshal did not quite know if he was playing the part of a sociopath, or being one in earnest. The captor removed the strip of tape from his captive's mouth. Nolan's skin smarted, but it could be the least of the discomfort he might endure.

"Who the fuck are you? Do you know who I am? What do you want?" the prisoner asked. His throat felt as rough as a matchhead.

"I have not brought you here to ask questions. You are here to answer them. Firstly, what is the number to unlock your phone?" Marshal said, withdrawing the device from his pocket. He had tried to access the phone back in Kilburn, but he needed the correct four-digit code.

Nolan pursed his lips and snorted. The enforcer's stony expression cracked a little. He appeared visibly torn. The messages and video on his phone would damn him. But being uncooperative might damn him in a different way.

"You've got the wrong man," Nolan insisted, unconvincingly.

"I'll be the judge of that. I know far more about you, Fergal, than you know about me. You may deem that as unfair, but we both know that life can be unfair," Marshal expressed. His voice was laced with both iciness and good humour. The hole in the balaclava around his mouth framed a polite, menacing smile. Nolan shifted in his chair once more – either unsettled, or he was testing the strength of his bonds. "Let me provide some evidence of how familiar I am with your history."

Marshal walked behind his prisoner once more and retrieved a small trolley, the kind one would find in a care home to help serve its bedridden residents. One of the wheels squeaked as he positioned it in front of Nolan, who gulped and wriggled in his chair again. The items on the trolley, laid out like surgical instruments, included a clawhammer, pliers, craft knife, a cordless drill and a can of lighter fluid.

"What is this?" Nolan said, with a modicum of confusion and innocence. Unconvincingly.

"I read one report which alleged that, when you tortured your victims with a clawhammer, you used one side on the left foot and the other on the right. Now, tell me your passcode," Marshal said, his tone as flat and blunt as the face of the hammerhead he picked up. "You have five seconds. One."

"I don't know what you're talking about."

"Two."

"This is fucking crazy. There's nothing on the phone."

"Three."

"Let's talk about this. We can come to an arrangement."

"Four."

"You don't know who you're dealing with."

Marshal sighed a little. Without saying a word, he placed the tape back over Nolan's mouth and smashed the flat end of the hammer against the prisoner's right foot three times. Bones cracked, snapping like sticks. With a flick of the wrist Marshal then turned the tool around and pounded the claw end of the hammer against Nolan's left foot with three powerful blows. Blood and sinew freckled the interrogator's balaclava. Nolan's foot was a giant wound. The white of bone could be seen through glistening flesh, like ancient gold coins glinting through the mud at an archaeological dig. A writhing Nolan let out a muffled threnody of screams and curses. Tears began to trickle down his rugged face. The Catholic, somewhat more lapsed than others, also offered up a prayer for mercy. But God seemed to have wax in his ears. Marshal was similarly impervious to the idea of forgiveness, his heart as hard as a mortuary slab. Cruelty, not clemency, was the order of the day.

He removed the tape. Nolan gunned out a stream of swear words, in between ululating and seething. The gangster, or businessman as he sometimes labelled himself, also breathlessly asked his torturer how much money he would accept to let him go. The bribe was then followed by a threat, and an appeal for mercy. Nolan revealed that he was going to be a father.

"A child needs a father," the Irishman half-asserted, half-sobbed.

"Jack Foster was a father. It is a pity you didn't feel that way a few weeks ago. You might not have then killed him and ended up here."

Blood vomited out of his left foot and then oozed, steadily. When Marshal picked-up the can of lighter fluid on the trolley, the numbers to his password started to pour out of Nolan's mouth, like compliments gushing from a sycophant. The interrogator asked a few follow-up questions concerning his relationship with his employers, John Mullen and Sean Duggan. The information helped to fill in some of the gaps in Mariner's files.

Marshal retreated behind his prisoner again and viewed the video of Foster's murder on the phone, which Nolan had recorded for his employer. Mullen had instructed his operative to delete the video, but Nolan had refrained from doing so. The sadist enjoyed re-watching the old soldier's torture and death. He also calculated that the video may come in handy in the future. He could blackmail Mullen over it one day or use it as a bargaining chip if ever he was pinched and in danger of being put away for a long stretch.

His face twitched a few times in response to the scenes on the screen, but for the most part Marshal remained seemingly dispassionate as he watched the abhorrent video. The balaclava made his head hot. The material began to irritate his scalp. But he kept it on. He took a breath, like an actor about to go on stage, and hit his mark once more in front of Nolan.

"Despite what your feet have recently endured, you can still walk away from this. I am happy to torture you until there is a united Ireland, but I have no desire to kill you, Fergal. Just give me the information I need. Tell me about the operation to abduct Foster. I am already familiar with some of the details – and I have just watched your video – so I will know if you are lying or keeping anything from me," Marshal sated, his voice sterner than before, his features tighter beneath the balaclava, as he picked up the can of lighter fluid and squirted half its contents over his captive, as if he were squeezing washing-up liquid all around a bowl.

Nolan whimpered and recoiled, as if the fluid had already turned into flames. The blood-soaked carpet soon became piss-soaked too. The interrogatee was in little doubt that, unlike threats made in an interview room by the police, the figure in front of him would make good on his word. Contrary to the literature *Freedernity* distributed, torture worked. Nolan clung to the hope that he would be able to survive the ordeal if he cooperated. If his captor intended to kill him at the end of the interrogation, after wringing him dry of information, he would not have concealed his face, the abductee reasoned. As wary as he might be in the future for having betrayed Mullen, Nolan was terrified of the blood-splattered tormentor who held his life in his hands right now.

The loyal republican began to talk. He even babbled on occasion. Mullen had received a signed and dedicated copy of *Thatcher's Willing Executioners* a week before the killing.

Duggan called Nolan over from Belfast, along with his niece and nephew. It did not take too long to track Foster down. They trailed their target for a day, partly to assess that the authorities had not assigned a security detail to him. Mullen decided to move quickly, lest Foster decided to flee the country or go into hiding. A team of four watchers coordinated to stalk their prey. Nolan remained, with two other men, in a van, a few minutes away, at all times - ready to close in. Foster's inebriated state on leaving the pub made it easy to abduct the ex-soldier. He was driven to an old IRA safehouse, just outside of Tring, in Buckinghamshire. The prisoner was tortured throughout the night. Nolan swore on the Bible that he had been but a spectator during the bloodletting, but Marshal had already seen evidence to the contrary during the video. Nolan also insisted that Mullen gave the order to execute Foster. "It was all Mullen. I was just following orders." After dumping the body on Herbert Crescent, which was reported to be Duggan's idea, the van was driven to a gypsy camp in Essex, which helped distribute drugs for the Real IRA, where it was disposed of.

The prisoner rambled on, divulging as much detail as possible. The more he talked, the less he would be tortured, he instinctively reasoned. It was understandably difficult to ascertain how satisfied his masked inquisitor was with his confession.

"Mullen has got his fingers in all sorts of pies. He's still in bed with the IRA, despite all the bollocks he comes out with on TV. He even headed up a funding trip to the US last year, on the condition that he was given ten percent of any money that was raised... Yes, Duggan took the shot from across the building to kill Byrne. I know where Duggan keeps his bug-out bag, with a stash of cash inside. Let me go and I'll tell you where it is. You can have it all..."

The ardent republican talked until his throat ran dry. Marshal offered his prisoner several mouthfuls of water, to remedy his rasping voice. The offer was gratefully accepted. The small act of kindness gave Nolan a small measure of hope. Surely, if his interrogator intended to kill him, he would not bother to give him water. In truth, Marshal had let Nolan drink in order to moisten his throat - so as to better understand what he was saying through his thick accent.

"I don't know anything more, my hand to God. If you let me go, I won't even tell Mullen about this," Nolan insisted, thinking how he would not rest until he caught-up with the man in front of him. He wanted the man standing over him to be sitting in the chair. Nolan would let his prisoner live, in order to torture him for longer. "I'll disappear."

"That you will," Marshal replied, emotionlessly, before removing his balaclava. He knew that by wearing the garment, Nolan might believe he would be released after his ordeal - if he cooperated. Marshal felt the slight temptation to torture his friend's killer for torture's sake. He could drill into his kneecap. Or chin. Or temple. But the soldier told himself that he wasn't a sadist.

"Don't kill me," Nolan pleaded, his eyes widening once more. Relieving his bladder once more. Wriggling in his chair once more. His voice cracking once more. All in vain.

The tape was placed over his mouth, for the last time.

Marshal walked around the back of his captive, wrapped his muscular right arm around Nolan's throat and crushed his windpipe, as the lightbulb began to flicker overhead. As he relentlessly tightened his hold Marshal pictured scenes from the video in his mind's eye. If Nolan somehow put up a fight, Marshal failed to notice.

There was still work to be done. He rolled the corpse up in the second-hand square of carpet he had bought and placed in the back of the van. He hauled the body out and lifted it over his shoulder. The vehicle was parked next to an abandoned wharf. The building was due to be demolished in a month's time. Mariner had recommended the location. Porter had forwarded the information on, without comment.

Gunmetal grey clouds congregated overhead, like a smack of jellyfish, as Marshal walked towards the end of a small jetty and dropped the body in the water, after fastening the dead man to some old dumbbells he owned. It was not the first corpse disposed of in the Thames. It would not be the last, either. A few bubbles rose to the surface just after the corpse was swallowed up by the murky river, as if it were burping after a meal.

He was diligent in cleaning the van, mindful of not leaving any trace evidence of Nolan. Of his crime. Sin. He heard the voice of Foster inside his head. *Better to be safe than sorry.* Marshal hoped that his friend was looking down on him, witnessing how he was fulfilling his promise. He did not know whether he felt half-redeemed or half-damned, as he smoked three cigarettes in succession after climbing into the cab of the vehicle.

Like a hand drawn to a flame, Marshal watched the video over again. Nolan had given up the names of his confederates, who had been present when his friend was murdered. One of the names, Kevin Morrison, had featured in the intelligence files, along with a photograph. Marshal recalled how Morrison possessed a protruding Mr Punch chin. Bushy, ginger eyebrows rested on his forehead like a couple of dead caterpillars. He had been arrested for smuggling contraband several years ago and a was person of interest in a series of recent car bomb attacks in Derry. Morrison was a mere foot-soldier, however.

Marshal was determined to work his way up, not down, the food chain.

15.

The day after Marshal returned from Kent, he contacted Oliver Porter. He wanted to start turning the screw on his target. Marshal briefly played out the scenario of forwarding the incriminating video onto the authorities. But how incriminating would it prove to be? It was now doubtful, to say the least, that the prosecution could call Nolan as a witness. There would be questions concerning the source of the evidence. Mullen could still claim plausible deniability. There was still no irrefutable proof that Nolan was acting on Mullen's orders. His alibi was still sound. The statesman would claim that the prosecution was a conspiracy and politically motivated. Knowing the furore that it could cause, the Crown Prosecution Service might even spike its guns and drop the case altogether. The accused might claim diplomatic immunity - or flee to a non-extradition country. There was more than one way that the fish could slip through the net. Mullen could elude both justice and vengeance, if the two were not one and the same thing. Marshal decided to pursue his own form of justice. He could still use the video to his advantage.

"You are playing with fire," Porter warned, after Marshal disclosed his strategy, as he tossed Violet another dog treat during their walk. It was a beautiful day, aside from the cloud his friend was casting over it.

"I'll need to, if I am going to smoke the bastard out. I have a plan, to reel in the fish."

"You know as well as I do, James. Man plans, God laughs."

Porter was tempted to enquire more into the events at the wharf. But he was wary of asking questions that he did not want to know the answers to. *I'm retired*, he told himself, more than once. He assented to Marshal's request, however, in recommending a journalist who would be willing to run a story on Mullen.

Towards the end of the call, Marshal asked after Grace. The first thing he had done, when returning from Kent, was check his phone for a message from his girlfriend. Or should he now call her his ex-girlfriend? If not for Foster's death, she might now be his fiancé. Grace was now becoming Gatsby's green light for Marshal. Distant. Part-fantasy.

"As much as I may be an admirer of Hartley's titular novel, I cannot act as a go-between for you and Grace. You should make the call. But you should not wait around forever to do so."

An unerring silence ensued. Porter even thought that the connection might be lost. At the other end of the line Marshal stared at his bare hand and imagined a wedding ring on his finger. Might it not cut into his skin like the ties he had placed around Nolan's wrists?

Grace had now swapped over a photo of the happy couple with one of the bookshop on her screensaver. She visited the store every day in an effort to stay busy, distracted. She received a barrage of messages, from the likes of Xanda Doleman and Nigel Raglan, asking her out to dinner. Grace neither accepted nor declined the offers.

John Mullen was about to find out, if he did not already know, that a week was a long time in politics. He turned his flabby hand into a flabby fist and, mallet-like, pounded his desk in frustration and rage. The measure of *Bushmills* in the tumbler was twice as normal. He had put his phone on silent due to the incessant ringing and pinging messages, although it still lit up and vibrated regularly.

Duggan paced up and down in a corner of the office, calling confederates in London and Belfast, enquiring as to the whereabouts of his cousin. He cursed his name more than once. He felt like killing him - if he wasn't dead already. His nose was screaming out for cocaine, like a child in a supermarket demanding sweets.

Several newspapers, tabloid and broadsheet alike, were strewn across the desk. Each headline rankled, knotting up the statesman's stomach.

"Sinn Fein politician uses taxpayer money to fund love nest with high-class prostitute... Tonight, Josephine... An escort with her John... DUP asks for enquiry into misuse of public money... Beauty and the Beast... Beauty call... Sinn Shame..."

Compromising photographs accompanied the articles. Photos of the couple leaving and entering their respective apartment blocks. They were kissing and holding hands in some. Josephine was picking crumbs of food from his chin in another. Mullen found himself reading some of the comments when he started going through some of the coverage online.

"She looks more like his daughter, or granddaughter... Is he about to kiss or eat her? It's sick. He's a pervert... I preferred it when he was in bed with the IRA... We need to clean out the Augean stables of Sinn Fein. My money should be used to pay for nurses, not for politicians to pay for tarts who dress up as nurses."

Mullen had received a call from a journalist, Trevor Giles, the evening before, asking if the politician would like to respond to the story before it went to print. It would be too late for his lawyer to try and slap an injunction on the story. Essentially the facts were correct, although that would not prevent the statesman from staunchly refuting the salacious claims. The photographs were particularly damning. Mullen was tempted to bribe or threaten the journalist, but he could not be sure if the call was being recorded, or if there were people listening in on the other end of the line.

Another call came through, this time in the middle of the night. It was from the party secretary, Allan Boyle. Mullen could remember when Boyle was a teenager, rattling a collection tin in the pubs, fundraising for the cause. He could also remember Boyle in his twenties, vomiting after witnessing his first kneecapping. The former university student, a self-proclaimed "Marxist and intellectual", was always keen to pen-push, rather than hold a gun as a volunteer. Boyle was a snivelling, cowardly bastard who had always felt uncomfortable and deficient in the company of the veteran campaigners, Mullen judged.

"You know that I do not care what you do in your private life. We all have our indulgences," Boyle remarked, sounding more like a Westminster mandarin than a docker's son from Belfast. Mullen thought to himself how Boyle's indulgences included paying rent boys and preferring singing the *Internationale* over any rebel song. "But the voters - and our donors - do care about such things. The party is going to have to suspend you, pending an investigation. We cannot allow our opponents to generate too much political capital out of this. The party and cause must come first. The wind will blow over eventually, however, and we can re-assess things then. You will understand that it will be best for everyone if we do not put you forward for selection when it comes to the next election."

A vein throbbed in Mullen's temple as his insipid colleague spoke. How dare the upstart, who would not be in the position he was in if not for the generation who came before him, lecture him on what was best for the party and cause! Mullen's nose grew redder then normal. He bit his tongue and ground his teeth. Mullen would not have been surprised if Boyle was behind the leaking of the material. It was no secret how Boyle wanted to usher the old guard out and turn the party into a socialist endeavour. It was strange, comical, that the party was willing to overlook his terrorist past and current criminal enterprises - but God forbid he take a mistress.

Duggan worked out that the photographs had been taken after the soldier's death. The Head of Security posed that there could be a connection - but could offer no other intelligence concerning the issue. The apparent disappearance of Nolan could surely not be a coincidence. His cousin would have had access to their employer's schedule, to arrange the photographs. The articles had also contained emails from Mullen, which condemned him as much as the photograph and lead story. Duggan judged that Nolan had been cc'd on the emails, some of which had been sent over a year ago. The emails had never been intended for public consumption. Mullen had described a rabbi as a "buck-toothed kike" and a health minister as a "mincing lefty". If Nolan was involved in the leak, he would not have acted alone, Duggan reasoned. He would have been bribed or coerced, but by who? There were more questions than answers. One such question was, if Nolan had been turned – did he still possess a copy of the video to pass on to the press or police?

Mullen had made too many enemies over the years to narrow candidates down to a single suspect. It was just as likely that the photos could have been arranged and leaked by a seeming ally. Sinn Fein had spent just as much time over the years in-fighting, as well as combating their opponents. Mullen would have been capable of destroying a rival in such a way, so why should others not be capable of such actions?

It was now midday. Mullen had just spent the past half an hour on the phone to his accountant. It was time to move more of his money into his offshore accounts, so the party, the authorities and his wife could not have access to his capital. He also instructed Duggan to call in some debts. "Don't accept any excuses. Punish anyone who is unable or unwilling to pay. We need a show of strength right now."

The politician mopped his brow and sipped, or more than sipped, his whiskey. He called his wife again. No answer. He then called his daughter again. No answer. Both before and after those calls, he rang Josephine. No answer. The statesman was not used to having his calls go unanswered. Mullen needed to speak to his mistress, to warn or pay her off so that she did not speak to the media and make a bad situation worse. He prayed for an earthquake or outbreak of war, somewhere in the world, to take the story off the front pages.

Email after email came in, like bullets spraying out of a machine gun. Talks that he had arranged were suddenly cancelled. He instructed Caitlin to keep any fees, if they had paid in advance. He was formally suspended from a couple of company boards he sat on. On being told by Caitlin that he was starting to receive a torrent of messages from his constituents, the statesman gnashed his teeth and lashed out:

"Fuck the fucking constituents. Those needy, whining bastards are the least of my concerns," he bellowed, before throwing a coffee cup across the room – and smashing a photograph of himself and Mo Mowlam which hung on the wall.

Mullen barely had time to think about the source of the betrayal or attack, let alone what he would do to the person or persons responsible. He was tempted at one point to unleash Duggan on the journalist behind the article. "Pay him or pull his teeth out. Just get me a name." But he changed his mind. Any move against Giles might prove the final nail in his coffin.

The sun was just about to set. The day had been long, as if stretched out upon a rack. For every fire he had tried to put out, two flared up. Mullen was sitting with his head in his hands when he glanced at his computer screen to see another email flash up. It was from a solicitor, one Adam Marcus. Marcus informed Mullen that his wife had engaged the law firm to commence divorce proceedings. He should not attempt to contact his wife. As much as it had strangely been a highlight of his day when he read the word "divorce", the words "financial settlement" had been less welcome.

Marshal had accessed Nolan's email and contacted Giles, playing the disgruntled employee who was owed money by his employer. Payback would now come in the form of ruining Mullen's reputation – and selling his story for cash (Giles transferred £10k into Nolan's bank account to buy the rights to the photos). Marshal forwarded on the photographs, along with a wealth of compromising emails.

Evening.

Mullen's foot tapped up and down beneath his desk. It did so when the politician was anxious or horny. His tie was askew. His grey complexion resembled parchment. The day had aged him more than the past year. Duggan had just discovered the payment from the journalist to his cousin. Nolan had ratted them out, for a measly ten grand. Or had he?

"My cousin still might not be behind things. Something else could be going on here," Duggan argued, not just in an attempt to defend his kinsman (and a potential error of judgement on his part). No one had seen hide nor hair of Nolan in the past twenty-four hours or so. He could have been used and disposed of. Disappeared.

"Well, do your damned job and find out who it is. Someone is fucking with me. We need to start fucking with them," the statesman raged, running his fingers through what little hair he had left. His hand trembled slightly as he poured himself another whiskey.

His chin buried itself into his chest as he slumped even further into his chair. The large, expensive *Eames* had once felt like a veritable throne. But Mullen's kingdom was crumbling around him. He felt more like he was in the stocks, than sitting on any throne. Money would soon be slipping through his fingers, like grains of sand. He once heard a celebrity call divorce the "love tax". Courtiers were not replying to his summons. His queen - and mistress - had abandoned him. How long before the tabloids found Josephine - and paid her thirty pieces of silver to crucify him? People were treacherous and cynical. It was what made them people. In the same way that he was calling in his debts, Mullen received a couple of calls from unofficial business partners. They were calling in debts that Mullen owed to them. It was a signal that he was no longer considered a good bet.

The shit-storm had no intention of abating, it seemed. There were still plenty of thunderclaps and lightning strikes to come, he imagined. Mullen tried to call Josephine again. He wanted to just hear her voice, as well as order her not to speak to the media. No answer.

A blister was forming on her palm from where she had gripped the carrying case too tightly throughout the day. The blaring lights of Cork airport hurt her eyes. She put her sunglasses on, again. The escort deliberately dressed unglamorously and wore her hair differently to how it had been in the photos. Several youths, who were part of a stag party, wolf-whistled at the woman. Josephine hoped that they would catch a dose of the clap. An ageing stewardess, with a tan as fake as her *Armani* watch, offered up a haughty or disapproving look - as if she had recognised the scarlet woman. In reply, Josephine replied with a defiant or scornful expression. She then thought how paranoia might be setting in. Had the stewardess really recognised her?

She had immediately packed some essentials that morning, after summoning the courage to speak to her mother - and request to come home. The call girl had first tried to get through to Luke (the hedge fund manager) and Jamahl (a DJ), hoping that one of them might take her in or pay for her to stay in a quiet, boutique hotel outside of London. No answer. Her nightmare was coming true. The escort had wanted to be rich, but she never wanted to be famous. Josephine turned her phone on silent, as call after call and message after message come in from private or unknown numbers. Some texts and voicemails offered escalating sums to sell her story. She was half-expecting former clients, who had been celebrities, to contact her - or sell their stories to secure a sixteenth minute of fame.

A few other old, creepy clients got in touch:

"I'm here for you."

When she heard the voicemails, calling her "Beauty", it made her skin crawl.

A couple of girls, also in the trade, offered their support. But, for most of her friends, their silence was deafening. It spoke for the equality of the sexes that women could be as heartless as men.

Josephine had made a promise to Mullen, as she had done so for her other clients, that she would always remain discreet about their time together. Others might not judge her to be honourable, but Josephine believed in keeping her word. "When you give your word, you must keep it," her father had told her when she was just a little girl. It would be bad for future business if she was seen as being indiscreet too.

Thankfully, she would be home by midnight. Josephine saw Mullen's number flash up once more. She was tempted to answer it. She had some sympathy for what he might be going through. It was likely that his career would be over. She liked him. But she did not like him that much - and ignored the call.

Instead, she sent a text message to her mother to say that she had landed safely. Her mother had avoided speaking about the affair over the phone. Her silence spoke volumes. Josephine was bracing herself for a lecture, or Catholic sermon, tonight or in the morning. The mother would doubtless tell her daughter that she had brought shame on the family - and herself. But she would also put her arms around her daughter and cook-up her favourite meal. Josephine was more worried about disappointing her father. She could no longer be daddy's innocent little girl. It would break her heart if she had somehow broken his - if he proved too embarrassed to go down the pub or look her in the eye. Her mother had said over the phone: "This could be a good thing for you. You can start over and train to be a nurse again."

Right now, it did not feel that a "good thing" was happening. Right now, it felt like whoever had taken those photographs had snatched her life away.

Josephine switched hands and continued to pull the carrying case behind her.

16.

The following day Mullen paid an inordinately expensive lawyer to counsel him to agree to any settlement that his wife's lawyer proposed.

"Whatever is on the table will be a better scenario to the dangers of contesting the settlement. You may need to give your wife half of your estate - or risk her taking it all. By all means hide what assets you can - but hide them well if you do."

The terrorist's instinct was to fight, but the strategy would have to be one of appeasement and consolidation. His wife would have the choice as to whether she took the house in Ireland or sold it. The "harpy" would likely demand a large lump sum, as well as act as a weeping sore by securing a monthly maintenance sum. Divorce proceedings should not turn into court proceedings. Further dirty laundry would be aired. Mullen judged that if he could circumvent his wife's lawyer and speak to her directly, he might be able to negotiate a more favourable settlement. His lawyer, who charged nine hundred pounds an hour (excluding VAT), understandably suggested that all correspondence should go through his office.

A different - but equally expensive - lawyer advised the statesman not to initiate legal action against any of the media, regarding the recent allegations. The damage was already done, and the lawyer delicately explained how it was unlikely that any action or injunction would succeed, because the allegations could be substantiated.

At the same time as Mullen was meeting with his lawyers, Duggan tried to get on the front foot. He first visited his cousin's flat. There was a distinct lack of evidence indicating that Nolan had planned to go on the run. Duggan found his passport in a bedside table drawer and a large roll of twenty-pound notes in a Celtic FC coffee mug. His clothes, as well as other possessions, were all present and accounted for. Duggan proceeded to pop into a couple of local pubs to ask after his cousin. They mentioned that they had last scene him a couple of days ago.

"Was everything normal with him?" Duggan asked.

"Well, he was drunk, if you could call that normal," one landlord replied, shrugging his shoulders whilst serving the tough-looking Irishman a pint of Guinness.

Following his employer's strict instruction, Duggan also visited Josephine's apartment building before returning to the office. He pulled out a few notes from Nolan's roll of cash and paid the concierge to grant him access to the escort's flat. There was a distinct wealth of evidence suggesting that Josephine had absconded – and would not be returning any time soon. The question was whether she was still in the capital or not. And would his employer think *good riddance* - or be obsessed with locating her? The Head of Security already believed that the escort had turned his friend's head too much. Women had always been Mullen's weakness. The whore had proved to be more trouble than she was worth. During the Troubles, the lieutenant was on constant alert, mindful that the security services could arrange a honey trap to compromise the senior IRA figure. As a young soldier, as Duggan deemed himself, he possessed a blind faith in his commander. He believed that Mullen could be a new Michael Collins. But Duggan had watched his mentor grow old. He had served closely enough with him to observe all his foibles and failures. The staunch republican now served under Mullen because he paid his wages. If Duggan was ordered to find the escort, he would do so with little zeal. *Let the bitch stay hidden*.

As the Irish enforcer sat in the back of the cab, glowering at Britain and the British out of the window, he envisioned catching up with the person behind the leak. He would put a single bullet in his head. The punishment for an informant. Duggan would be more than willing - it would be a pleasure - to torture the culprit beforehand. He licked his lips and his stony expression briefly cracked at the prospect. It was an art form, or science, to torture a man to within an inch of his life. It was like dangling a man over a precipice and then pulling him back at the last moment, only to repeat the process again and again. Duggan grunted to himself, more than once, in the back of the vehicle. He craved another Guinness, or something stronger. He sniffed and snorted, keen to scratch the itch of being violent, for violence's sake.

When the Head of Security returned to the office, he ran another sweep for any listening devices. Just after he did so Caitlin walked in, to pass on a message to her employer.

"Not now," Mullen barked, flashing his jaundiced teeth.

The unfairly chastised secretary returned to her desk and resumed her search for a new job.

Duggan sat down, after daring to pour himself a large *Bushmills*, and proceeded to update his employer. There were still more questions than answers, frustratingly.

"It's looking unlikely that Nolan is behind all this, or that he's working for someone else. But let us just pretend that he has fucked us over. He would still have a copy of the video he made - and sent you on the night when we dealt with Foster. Why hasn't he been in touch to blackmail you over the video?"

"Maybe he realises that if he released the video, he would be incriminating himself. The footage would damage him more than me. I can deny involvement still, but he has a starring role," Mullen posed. "But you're probably right. It doesn't fit that Nolan is behind all this shit. The question is, if your cousin was taken - does the bastard who took him have a copy of the video? Would they not have passed it onto the police or press by now? Or been in touch to blackmail me?"

"We could be dealing with the scenario that Nolan deleted the video, or whoever disappeared him accidentally disposed of the phone. You might be lucky."

"I don't feel that lucky at the moment. If I fell in a bed of roses at the moment, I'd come up smelling of shit. But you might be right."

Mullen got to his feet and moved to the window. He could see but not hear the gaggle of press outside the entrance to the building through the bulletproof glass. Should he have opened the window and stuck out his head then Mullen would have seen a couple of TV trucks decamped down the street. He peered down, his chubby features curdling with contempt, and gnawed on his nicotine-stained fingernails. The litigious terrorist has scoured the newspapers - print and online articles - hoping to find something libellous and actionable. He wanted to hurt them, silence them, sue them, if he could. But, for once, there was no fake news, as they brought up both his past and present sins. Mullen was still keen to get his own story out there. Perhaps he could reach out to Toynbee. He would probably be able to run a sympathetic, counter narrative in *The Guardian*. He could hint at a government conspiracy. Or the enemies of the peace process could be implicated. He could throw some red meat to his supporters and attack Boris Johnson. He just needed a journalist he could trust. He was more likely to find an honest politician.

Vultures.

The same people he had fed stories and leaks to were now feeding off him.

Parasites.

Earlier on in the day the hounded MP had barged through the throng of clicking cameras and badgering questions.

"No comment... Fake news," Mullen had said, whilst wishing he could tear off all the camera lenses pointing in his direction.

The crime boss, not averse to being part of a kleptocracy, thought of the hourly rate his lawyer was charging him again and glowered through the window, as if his eyes were trying to burn a hole through the thick glass. If his sins were somehow catching up to him, the statesman was willing to sin some more if it meant avoiding his fate and defeating his enemies.

*"It's the end of the world as we know it.
I feel fine."*

An eighties music shuffle played in the background as Marshal cradled a large brandy and sat on the sofa. He closed his eyes, tired from being glued to a laptop screen, and pinched the bridge of his nose, hoping the gesture would fend off a headache. He smoked a cigarette, not caring if he drifted off to sleep, burned his home down and died. He thought of Grace, which seemed to both soothe and stress his soul at the same time. On more than one occasion Marshal and Grace had stayed home for the evening, listening to music they wanted to share, whilst drinking to their heart's content – and making love afterwards. They would pick a decade, artist or genre and create a playlist for one another. Often, they would listen to country music. Marshal would put together a selection including Hank Williams, Jimmie Rodgers and Glen Campbell. As with other things, Grace helped bring Marshal up to date, introducing him to more modern artists. They both loved Dolly Parton. They were only human. He would have given up almost anything to be with Grace now, her body warming his on the sofa. Almost anything. Marshal could not give up his promise to kill John Mullen.

Let him sweat, Marshal thought, as he resisted the urge to contact his target and initiate the next phase of his plan. Once he ended Mullen's life he could get back to his own. Get back with Grace. But work still needed to be done, in relation to intelligence gathering. After resting his eyes, Marshal ran another search on Mullen, to measure the damage done already. The Irishman's wife had initiated divorce proceedings, which would help break the bank rather than her husband's heart. The party had suspended the veteran statesman. Further inquiries would be launched. Most political careers end in failure. However, Mullen's fall would be greater than others. Marshal watched the clip once more on the news of Mullen's arriving at his offices that morning. The once self-confident, self-important Sinn Fein stalwart appeared riled and distressed. He looked like he needed a drink, or already had had one too many. The more misery Mullen experienced, the better. But there was still a coffin-shaped hole in Marshal's breast. The soldier would not rest until one of them was in the ground. Every day that Mullen lived was an affront to decency. He was a black cloud in an otherwise grey sky. Every day that Mullen lived was a reminder that Marshal had failed to keep his promise.

"Working hard to get my fill
Everybody wants a thrill
Payin' anything to roll the dice
Just one more time
Some will win, some will lose
Some were born to sing the blues."

Marshal stubbed out another cigarette, balancing it on top of the others, funeral pyre-like, in the ashtray. He heard a dog bark outside a few times. For a moment he thought it sounded like Violet, Porter's mongrel. Marshal mused how he would have liked to have seen the ebullient dog, but not necessarily her owner. He recalled the week when he and Grace had looked after Violet when Porter and his wife had been on holiday. It struck Marshal how he could not remember a more enjoyable, contented week in his life. They had behaved like a young, married couple. He had not been as happy in the army, nor during his carefree days as a bachelor, when he had smoked to his lung's content.

Marshal checked his phone again for a message from Grace. Nothing. The screen was obdurately blank, like a broken TV. The dull ache swirled and swelled, like hunger pangs.

17.

Marshal woke. Another day. Another dolour.

For a moment he believed that if he rolled over, he might see Grace lying beside him.

He felt like he was no longer laughing at life. Rather, life was laughing, scornfully, at him. His tongue felt furry and fat, lying in his mouth like a lazy cat. He wanted to drink both a bottle of water and a bottle of mouthwash, after the previous night's bout of cigarettes and alcohol.

Thankfully, or not, Marshal still felt the itch to assassinate Mullen. Revenge still flickered in his eyes, like a flame, shortly after he woke. A dull ache still gnawed at his innards - yet the feeling nourished him at the same time. He showered and smoked and then took out his gun. He cleaned the Glock 21 once more, as if to prove his mettle - to himself and an onlooking Foster - that he was still sincere in fulfilling his vow. The paratrooper was ready for anything. Ready for action, like Hamlet after returning from his voyage to England.

Marshal gripped the loaded pistol. He - and the weapon - were a coiled spring. Sooner or later, both would need to be unleashed. The soldier was tempted to take the weapon with him, as he reconnoitred the area of the offices in Mornington Crescent. He flirted with the prospect of accidentally bumping into Mullen and his Head of Security in a side street. Gunning them down.

The soldier remembered the second time he had killed someone, in Helmand province. He was taking part in a routine patrol of a village, after delivering a consignment of aid. The aid workers, from DFID, with their typical "can't do" attitude, had called their union and refused to leave the camp to deliver the supplies. They cited that the temperature was too hot to work in, but really they considered leaving the compound too dangerous. Marshal was accompanied by a young squaddie, Billy Turney, from Wolverhampton. Turney was still fresh-faced, with cherubic features - but he swore like the devil. He had followed his older brother into the army. He was hoping to make some money and learn a trade - and to buy a house in the Midlands and marry his sweetheart, Melanie. Turney was just a month into his tour, still excited and anxious in equal measure. One day he was expecting to take part in a movie-like firefight, the next he was half-paralysed with fear, expecting to be fired upon at any moment. Marshal recalled how the youth's family used to send him regular care packages, filled with fruit flavoured vape capsules, Andy McNab paperbacks and boxes of Liquorice Allsorts. Turney was mid-swear word, talking about Gordon Brown, when the two men walked around into a side street and encountered two Afghanis. The first, wearing a kaftan, was as young and fresh-faced as Turney. Abdul. He was carrying a school satchel over his shoulder, with wires spilling out of it. In his right hand he carried an old hunting rifle. The second man, Hamid, was older, with an unkempt beard. His claw-like fingers gripped a Kalashnikov, with some Arabic script scrawled into the wooden stock. The older man was mentoring the younger on setting an IED. The encounter was happenstance. Time stood still, and for a moment the world no longer seemed to spin on its axis. But for only a moment. The older men reacted before the younger. Hamid raised his rifle, intending to cut down both infidels with a brief spray of bullets. Killing was Allah's work - and he was a good Muslim, he believed. The veteran Taliban soldier was quick. But not quick enough. Marshal, as if realising he was taking part in a gunfight, was faster on the draw. His weapon came to life, yet he tamed its wriggling report. He didn't hesitate, and he didn't miss.

Three small plumes of smoke exhaled out of Hamid's chest. Abdul remained paralysed with shock. As wide-eyed as a doll. Seemingly innocent. His weapon appeared limp in his hands. Marshal could have apprehended the enemy. The adolescent could have been a source of intelligence, concerning the Taliban forces in the area. Abdul could have been reasoned with. Emancipated. Marshal only expended a solitary bullet, fired into his throat, to take out the youth. His expression was the soul of dispassion. Turney glanced at his fellow paratrooper, as if he were a stranger. Blood freckled the sandy ground.

"I am not usually given to quoting or agreeing with Keynes, but in the long run we are all dead," Marshal remarked, when someone asked him why he killed the young Afghan, as opposed to allow him to surrender.

Marshal mentored the squaddie for a while. He taught him how to control his emotions, instead of letting his emotions control him. He advised him on how to best rehydrate and conserve energy in the unforgiving heat. He gave him a few books – Lee Child, Steven Saylor and Richard Foreman – to read. He taught him how to shoot. To kill. Unfortunately, Turney suffered an injury - from an IED - and returned home, shortly before his tour was due to end. The last Marshal had heard, he was trying to get together the money to set-up a small courier business in Wolverhampton.

Marshal envisioned encountering his current enemies in a side street, from happenstance or otherwise. He would be happy for his target to suffer the same fate as the Taliban he had killed. More than happy.

It was a fine day, far sunnier than his mood. Marshal sat in the coffeeshop across from the main entrance to Mullen's office building, casually reading a newspaper. The news was dull or depressing, intended to polarise and provoke. Human interest stories held little interest, though. Marshal regretted not bringing a book along, though he feared being too engrossed and not focussing on the task at hand.

Mullen pulled up in his black Lexus, just half a dozen yards from the doorway to the building. The pugnacious-looking driver was more than just a driver. He was a former paramilitary. Armed. Dangerous. Duggan exited the vehicle first. He surveyed the street, before accompanying Mullen inside. Marshal noted how they were met with another member of their security detail in the lobby of the glass-fronted ground floor. Mullen's offices took up the entire top floor of the converted municipal building. Attempting to storm the castle and confront his targets in the lobby, or on the upper floor, was not an option. Marshal was conscious of not wanting to put any civilians in a potential crossfire.

An hour later Duggan left the building, on his own. He paced up and down the street, fidgeting whilst talking on the phone. Marshal noted the bulge from the gun beneath his suit jacket. Ten minutes later he was met by an ill-dressed, lank-haired teenager on a bicycle. With little ceremony Duggan handed over a few notes, in exchange for the youth giving him a bag or two of cocaine. Blink and one would have missed the transaction. Marshal rolled his eyes. He briefly wondered if Duggan's habit was making him more paranoid than usual - and if that was a good or bad thing in relation to the task at hand. Marshal mused that Porter was right. Any plan to kill Mullen needed to factor in Duggan. He would need to get past, or go through, the brutal enforcer. Marshal also did not want to look over his shoulder after killing Mullen, lest the loyal lieutenant took it upon himself to track down his friend's executioner, as Marshal had avenged Foster's death.

Duggan went back inside. Marshal checked a few news feeds and came a across a couple of reports that Mullen was planning to return to Belfast at the end of the week, "to resolve mounting personal and professional issues". The news was a call to arms. Marshal could not afford to let his target fall out of sight. A formidable task would be made doubly difficult if he had to pursue Mullen into unfamiliar territory. His name might be flagged up to the likes of Coulson if he travelled to Belfast and the suspect in Foster's murder was assassinated there. Mullen could even disappear altogether after settling various affairs in Belfast. The chances of locking his target into his sights would recede like the tide and he would, Cnut-like, be powerless to prevent it.

He yawned - whilst glancing over a story in the newspaper about a Tory politician working with a senior union official to embezzle funds from an NHS Trust - and determined that it was now, or never. Marshal would make the call later. Pull the trigger and scratch the itch.

When he returned to Amelia St, Marshal felt a different type of itch. Partly he was tired of bloody images of Foster's torture and execution spooling through his mind, like a snuff movie. He no longer wanted to picture Mullen's bloated, pompous features either. He wanted to think about Grace. His thumb hovered over the buttons on his Blackberry, tempted as he was to send a message. He missed the way she slow-cooked lamb, and how she could tell when he was being sarcastic, but others couldn't, when they were at a party. He missed watching movies - *Wall-E* and *Onegin* - with Grace. He missed signing off each text with her with *xx*. When he was posted in Helmand, Marshal had occasionally dreamed about having someone to come home to. The dream had come true. But it might soon fade. Die. Marshal realised that if he could not marry Grace, he would not marry anyone.

Marshal cradled a whisky tumbler one hand and his Glock in the other. Hank Williams and the sound of a pedal steel guitar played in the background. Melancholy infused the air like cigarette smoke. The gun felt as heavy as his heart. The loaded gun. Marshal idly wondered how many cells in his body would be willing to turn the weapon on himself. Not enough would be one answer. But more than zero would be another. He glanced at the copy of the Graham Greene biography on his coffee table and re-read a passage in the book:

"I put the muzzle of the revolver into my right ear and pulled the trigger. There was a minute click, and looking down at the chamber I could see that the charge had moved into the firing position. I was out by one... My heart knocked in its cage, and life contained an infinite number of possibilities. It was like a young man's first successful experience of sex."

Marshal wryly smiled, thinking that it would be somewhat difficult to play Russian Roulette with a Glock. He pictured the revolver, contained in Foster's holdall. He wondered if the bag contained any ammunition for the weapon. Playing Russian Roulette would be one of the only sources of an adrenaline rush, to rival the soldier's time in Helmand. Would he ever be courageous, depressed or foolish enough to place a bullet in the gun, spin the wheel, and pull the trigger? Suicide was an answer. But Marshal did not want to ask the question. He needed to stay alive long enough to do his duty by Foster. He needed to use the bullets with Mullen's and Duggan's names on them before he could consider firing upon himself.

It was time to make the call.

Marshal sat on a wooden bench in a quiet corner of Geraldine Mary Harmsworth Park, or Bedlam Park as it was often called, named after the site of the famous, or infamous, mental hospital once situated there. He pulled out a burner phone - along with a gizmo which Mariner sent to disguise his voice - and dialled the number he had pulled from Nolan's device.

Mullen sat behind the desk, too enervated even to drink. His daughter had just sent him a message, asking him to stop contacting her. He could not be sure if she was distancing herself from him for political or personal reasons. Mullen yearned for another Roy Greenslade, someone who could tell his side of the story. He needed a journalist who was as scrupulous, or rather unscrupulous, as a politician.

The phone which he used for his less official business, vibrated. The number was unrecognised, and the politician declined to answer.

Marshal was unsurprised and undeterred that he could not get through immediately. He sent a text message, however, to attract Mullen's attention:

I have information about Fergal Nolan and the contents of his phone.

The Irishman's tired eyes widened. His fleshy features even seemed to firm up a little, in anxiety or malice, as he read the message. Such was the dramatic change in his expression that Duggan stopped swiping right on the dating app, devoted to teenagers, that he was viewing.

A minute passed, during which Mullen showed the message to his lieutenant, before Marshal's burner phone rang.

"Who's this?" the statesman uttered, unable to suppress his contempt. His voice gruff and guttural.

Marshal kept his emotions in check, like taming the report of a gun, hearing the voice of the man responsible for his friend's murder. The man who he would kill.

"You do not need to know my name. You need to know that I have it in my purview to be your best friend or worst enemy. We are both aware that, as a politician, you like to talk. But you must now listen. I do not want you to take what I have to say personally. What I will be proposing is a business transaction. I have something in my possession that I would like to sell - and you would like to purchase. You will be tempted to ask a number of questions, which I can largely pre-empt and answer now. You would like to know how I acquired my information. Let's just say that you may have been right - and the intelligence services can be as corrupt as those they surveil. A member of one of the organisations, tasked with investigating you, alerted me to your various misdemeanours. He also flagged-up Fergal Nolan as being a potential weak link in your network. I can tell you that, in perhaps more ways than one, Nolan spilled his guts. He may have happily pocketed his thirty pieces of silver, by way of the pension plan that your company fails to pay. Or you may wish to conclude that Nolan is dead – and all that's left of him is a ring of scum, from him having taken an acid bath. But the fate of your former employee should be of little concern. It's in the past. What should concern you now is your future."

Mullen's rubbery lips were twisted, as if he might snarl at any moment. Yet his jaw was clamped shut. His face grew as red and hot as chipotle chilli as he listened to the arrogant, self-satisfied, distorted voice on the phone. Mullen attempted to interject, but the blackmailer calmly warned him not to interrupt. Duggan was equally affronted by the figure on the other end of the phone, but focused on scribbling down some notes on who their suspect might be.

Professional blackmailer/criminal... Links to intelligence services... Current MI5 or Met Police operative?... Fergal likely dead.

Marshal would have been satisfied to read Duggan's notes. The fox was throwing the hound off the scent.

"Another question you may have, is what am I doing this for? The dull but honest answer is money. For all the talk of social justice and need for climate change, money still makes the world go around. I do not hold any personal enmity against you. What I am proposing is a simple trade. You must remove emotion from any decision, as I have. I trust that I have gained your attention by selling certain titbits of information to the press. That was but an appetiser. The main course would be passing on the red meat of a video I have in my possession. I could have given the video to the media or your enemies if my intention was just to hurt you. But where would the profit be in that? My price, to hand over the phone and vanish, is simple and non-negotiable. Three hundred thousand pounds. To be paid tomorrow, at two o'clock. I will collect the money, which should be placed in a briefcase, from the reception of your offices. If you leave the case under the name of Dominic Usher. It will amuse me no end if you would like to google that name, in order to uncover my identity. My associate will put the phone in a padded envelope and hand it to the receptionist, to pass on to you. I imagine that you will be tempted to now threaten me - or refuse to pay. But I can assure you that everyone pays, in one way or another. I have sufficient information about your financials to suggest that the sum I require will not ruin you. It would be counter-productive to ask for an amount that you would be unable or unwilling to pay. I am a businessman, and a businessman must employ utmost good faith. I am an honest blackmailer - if that is not a contradiction in terms - far more honest than any of your colleagues in parliament. Once you make the payment, I will disappear into the ether. That will conclude our business. Please do not insult my – and your - intelligence - and argue that you will not be able to raise the requisite funds in time. For the fee of three hundred thousand pounds, I am letting you get away with murder. I am confident that you will accept the settlement, rather than face the consequences. Quite rightly, you would not believe me if I said that I will destroy all copies of the videos. But I will be retaining a copy for reasons of insurance, not to blackmail you a second time. I have no desire to tarnish my reputation and break my word."

Mullen seethed. Air whistled through his nasal hair. The statesman was a man accustomed to dictating instructions, not being dictated to.

"Even if you find the smallest, darkest hole to hide in, I will hunt you down for the dog that you are, should you attempt to double-cross me. You say you know me, but if you really knew me - and what I am capable of - you would not have targeted me. If I choose to, I could end you," the former Brigade Commander asserted, puffing out his chest, as if the blackmailer were present and ripe for intimidation.

"I suggest you concentrate on paying rather than threatening me. It is only natural for you to consider that I will use my leverage once more - and come back to extort money out of you once more, as you repeatedly extorted money out of people in Belfast during your previous career. But I never feed on a carcass more than once. If you endeavour to try and track me down, however, I will take great pleasure in chewing you up and spitting you out. Finding me will not be the end to your troubles, but the beginning of them," Marshal warned, his tone as polished and hard as steel.

His foot tapped nervously away on the bench. He felt like a bowstring, being drawn back too much, waiting to snap. Marshal wasn't sure how long he could keep up the act of playing the confident blackmailer. He gazed at the Imperial War Museum, which sat at the other end of the park. His grandfather had originally brought him to the museum when he was six. Marshal also remembered how he had taken Grace there on a date, some time ago. He had opened up to her, more than any of his other girlfriends, about his time as a soldier during the afternoon.

"I feel like I put the person I was in Helmand into a box - and put it in a corner of the attic - like packing away a toy soldier. I might sometimes want to unpack him, as though he needs to see the light of day once in a while. But not when I am with you... I much prefer mobilising the English language and unsheathing a quip rather than firing any weapon nowadays."

She had bought him a framed print of the iconic photograph - of Churchill holding a Tommy Gun - in the giftshop. The picture was still hanging on his bedroom wall. Marshal now felt a desperate desire to see Grace, to smell her perfume. He wanted to see her and hear her laugh more than capture Mullen in his crosshairs. He could no longer picture the engagement ring he had picked out.

Marshal reiterated the payment details and arrangements to conclude their transaction, before hanging up.

The die was cast.

18.

The neck of the whiskey bottle clinked against the rim of the glass as his hand trembled, in rage or anxiety, whilst pouring a drink. Mullen left the top off, both because he thought he might find it difficult to replace, and he would need to pour another measure soon. He puffed his cheeks out and exhaled. The former terrorist was resigned to paying, which was not to say he was happy about it. The blackmailer had already arguably ruined his career and marriage. Perhaps he should thank his tormentor for the latter. Mullen had twisted his wedding ring from his finger. His liver-spotted hand appeared better for it, he thought. He remembered how a few women had spurned his advances in the past, having seen the gold band. Or they were frigid, he judged. Mullen briefly wondered what Josephine would think, in relation to his prospective divorce. He also wondered if he would see her again.

Mullen instructed Caitlin to purchase a large briefcase, immediately. He made a call to his accountant and bank and moved some money around – money which he had intended to conceal from his disloyal spouse. Perhaps paying the blackmailer would start less than paying his wife. It stuck in Mullen's craw, to be pressured into paying. The former extortioner, during his days fund-raising for the cause, did not enjoy being extorted. Towards the end of their call the blackmailer had second-guessed his victim:

"Do not attempt to track the suitcase. Do not attempt to follow my associate. Should you do so, this will break the terms of our arrangement - and you will cause the outcome which you are trying to prevent. You need to swallow any pride or resentment you might be feeling - and pay the money. And it will then all be over."

Mullen noticed a couple of flies swirl around a wastepaper bin in the corner. The hum of their wings was even more vexing than the incessant drone of the air conditioning. He felt like ordering his lieutenant to dispose of the insects, as a prelude to swatting away his enemy. Mullen was not willing to be resigned to defeat completely, though. It was the man who was making his life a misery who needed to pay a price. The ultimate price.

"It's not all over. Far from it. The bastard thinks that he's thought of everything, but he's overconfident - and he has underestimated us. As you say, for all his talk of associates he could just be a lone wolf. If we take away the man, we take away the problem. He can be the new Tom Byrne. Walk into this lion's den and you'll get mauled. I want you to go over any intelligence files you have of potential suspects again. Post yourself on the roof opposite. If you have a target and shot, take it."

Duggan nodded - and sniffed. He would clean his sniper rifle this evening. It had been a long time since he had fired the weapon. Too long.

Hank Williams played in the background.
"No matter how I struggle and strive,
I'll never get out of this world alive."
The breeze billowed out the curtain. He took another sip of whisky, savouring the elixir as if it might be his last measure. Marshal smiled to himself. He thought how he was more nervous about the prospect of calling Grace, than he had been about talking to Mullen. Also, unlike his call to Mullen, Marshal struggled to compose his lines beforehand or know which persona to adopt. Be yourself, he could have advised. But who

was he? Soldier or civilian? Marrier or murderer? Someone who drunk too much, or not enough?

But Marshal had to talk to her. Before it was too late.

Grace could hear the nearby refrain of "stroke" coming from a procession of boats gliding down the nearby Thames. Gulls carped in the background too. She was home alone, again. Her fine eyes were a little puffy from crying, again. A half-empty, sweating bottle of Sancerre sat on the coffee table, just about within reach, as she lay on her leather sofa. Her head rested on a plump, plush cushion. Her knees were tucked-up, in the foetal position. The décor in the room - which looked out upon a neat, fragrant garden - was homely, elegant and expensive. Visitors gushed about her beautiful her home was. It was a dream house. But it increasingly left her cold. Rather than the walls closing in, she began to realise how large the house was, just for one person. Grace had finished furnishing all the rooms to her taste and satisfaction. But something was missing.

She let the phone continue to ring, both glad and stressed to see the caller ID flash up. Grace was more than tempted to let things go to voicemail. Why shouldn't she ignore him? Had he not ignored her? He had hurt her - and the former model had promised herself, on the flight from New York to London, that she would no longer put herself in a position to be hurt by a man again. For so long Marshal had not hurt her. Grace had to admit that he may not be the man she knew, or thought she knew. And their - or his - problem could not just be put down to the death of his friend. There was more to the story than that.

"Hi," Marshal said.

Grace initially paused, as she sat up straight on the sofa. She briefly wondered whether his "Hi" had been apologetic, sad, conciliatory. His greeting hung in the air, like a piece of mouldy cheese, on the turn.

Marshal stared at his Glock perching on a bookcase, by his collection of Loeb Classics. Plutarch, Cicero, Martial, Marcus Aurelius, Virgil and Horace sat next to one another, like a council of elders.

Grace wanted to cry - but did not quite know why.

"Hello," she finally replied. Her greeting was neutral, barely polite. But just about polite, like a housewife dealing with a tardy tradesman. She was relieved to hear his voice, though.

"Sorry that I haven't been in touch. Mea culpa. I could of course babble on like an idiot over the phone. But I'd prefer to babble on like an idiot in person. Can we meet?"

Grace wanted to be terse and unforgiving, but she liked it when Marshal was self-effacing. The dry-humoured soldier was a breath of fresh air compared to other men she had known. The fashion designers, actors, and financiers. The egotists, narcissists, and sociopaths.

"Yes," she replied, her voice as cold and hard as obsidian.

Another strained pause ensued. Marshal was not quite sure if it was indeed Grace on the other end of the call for one, brief, moment. He felt an all too familiar loathing for himself, swelling like goitre - for his specific sins and the general sins of man. Man is born into sin, as the sparks fly upwards. What progress can the pilgrim truly make?

"Would you be free to meet at Bobo at eleven tomorrow?"

Grace was minded to decide the time and the place of their meeting. She was owed that, at the very least. But she would assent. She was free - and wanted to see him.

Marshal was tempted to make a joke that he would have Chef serve him a slice of humble pie or make him eat crow - but desisted.

A short pause.

"I will be there. I have to go now. There is somebody at the door," Grace said, lying. Perhaps she said it to make him jealous, or to convey that she had already moved on. Grace was determined not to show how hurt she was. She would only be willing to do so in order to hurt him in return. Marshal was right when he quoted Homer, Grace mused.

Men are wretched things.

19.

Even the moreish smell of cooked bacon was unable to prompt Marshal to order some food as he sat in Bobo. He was early - keen not to add the misdemeanour of tardiness to his already blotted copybook. His innards felt uncommonly unsettled. Marshal could not quite decide if the butterflies in his stomach were borne from the nerves of meeting Grace - or murdering Mullen. He frequently straightened the gleaming cutlery in front of him, despite the items being arrow straight already. His eyes flitted from left to right, keeping an eye out for Grace. He was dressed smartly, in a summer suit, and had even ironed a shirt. He appeared as jittery as a man who was about to propose. But he was not about to propose. Far from it.

Grace approached, walking through the park. Did the sun come out even more? The skirt on her summer dress swayed, from the breeze or her brisk gait. She did not want to be impolite or late either. A ribbon of red lipstick made her already kissable lips glisten. She was Shania Twain, Dolly Parton and Julie Christie all rolled into one. Grace was beautiful. Marshal could have believed in Keats right now, that "beauty is truth, truth beauty." And in Dostoyevsky - "Beauty will save the world." The pedal steel guitar of his soul sang once more. Marshal temporarily forgot that he was intending to assassinate a man later in the day. His hand brushed against his cutlery, creating a lack of symmetry in front of him, but he didn't care. Pati, no stranger to style herself, complimented Grace on her dress before showing her to the table. Her heels clicked against the waxed wooden floor, as rhythmic and seductive as a flamenco dancer.

Marshal courteously stood up as Grace arrived. Perhaps courtesy, even more than beauty, could save the world.

"Hi," Grace said, somewhere in between warm and wistful.

"Hi," Marshal replied. He felt like half-smiling but forced a full smile. The usually articulate soldier did not quite know what to add. There was much he wanted to say. Too much. He had a novel's worth of words stuck in his throat. Or several novels. A romance. A tragic romance. A Graham Greene "entertainment". Marshal was unsure as to how the meeting would play out. More to the point, he was unsure how he wanted it to play out. He straightened his cutlery once more, albeit it was not as straight as before. He caught the scent of her perfume. His being shuddered - like the bus outside, stationary at the lights, juddered. If it shook any more, bits might fall off it.

The couple, if they could still be called a couple, ordered some coffees. They spoke about the weather and general, strained pleasantries, while waiting for their drinks. Marshal stirred his coffee for an elongated time, before leaning forward and speaking in earnest. Part of him wanted to reach out and hold Grace's hand. Part of him wanted Grace to reach out and hold his hand. Instead, he moved the pepper closer to the salt.

"You know me better than most, for better or worse," he remarked, with a furrowed brow, thinking how, from a certain point of view, she did not know him at all. "You know that something is wrong. But what's wrong?"

Nothing and everything, Marshal mused.

Grace had come with the intention of punishing Marshal for his risible behaviour. The former officer had not been a gentleman. But a sense of pity, rather than punitiveness, flooded her heart as she gazed at him from across the table. As much as he had shaved and was well-attired, weariness dripped from his features like dirty sweat. His eyes bespoke of a lack of sleep and surfeit of alcohol. He had somehow fallen - and was still falling, she sensed.

"You need to tell me, James. I think John's death triggered something that was already inside of you. The things that we bury have a way of rising to the surface at some point."

Marshal briefly wondered how long it would take for the dumbbells, holding Fergal Nolan down, to rust sufficiently - allowing his corpse to float to the surface.

"I know," he mumbled by way of a reply, like a chastened child, as he stared into his treacle-black beverage.

"You have grown so distant that I do not recognise you anymore. I was with you, but on my own, after John passed. You looked through me, rather than at me."

"I know. I'm still a little lost. I'm not sure if I know which are the right questions to ask, let alone what are the answers to such questions," Marshal said, his brow furrowed even more. He was tempted to offer up a "truth," that he had not wholly come back from the war, all those years ago. Jack was just one of many ghosts, he could have explained. He had seen too much death. His distance had come from him being damaged - and wanting to protect Grace. Yet the "truth" would have been, at best, a half-truth. He had not witnessed enough death. He wanted to take more lives. Marshal wanted revenge, not absolution. Should Grace know the whole truth about him, then she would not want to know it. If only men and women could be reconciled with lying to themselves and each other, then they might have a chance at living happily ever after, he wryly fancied. But perhaps they are reconciled to such rabid deception and self-delusion. It's the human condition, to deceive.

When Grace moved into his home, Marshal started to miss certain aspects of his old life. But when she moved out, he missed her. This meeting was partly about conveying to Grace that he loved her, more than he had loved any other woman.

Even if he had to leave her, she should know that he loved her. Ardently and devoutly. It was also about closure - saying goodbye - lest he not survive the day. But at the same time did he not want to leave the door open, so he could walk back through it tomorrow? If there was a tomorrow...

"Oliver said that I should be patient. But as much as I try to be a good Catholic, I do not have the patience of a saint," Grace half-joked, without smiling. "I do not think there is, but if there is someone else, you must tell me."

It was Grace's turn to dolefully stare into her coffee.

"No one else would be foolish enough to have me. But there's no one else," Marshal replied, assuredly, rightly despising himself for having caused Grace to suffer such tortuous thoughts. There was someone else, though, he considered. The fashion model's rival was a porcine, ignominious terrorist. Marshal noted that he owed Porter a debt of gratitude, for fighting his corner, but ultimately, he would need to fix things himself.

Another pregnant pause. Marshal subtly checked his watch. Grace pretended not to notice that Marshal had checked his watch.

The sound of a nearby diner breaking a glass shattered the shard of silence between them.

Mike, the owner of Bobo, rolled his eyes - again. As his attention was drawn towards the sound, he noticed Marshal and Grace and headed over to say hello. Mike would be duly discreet about how many times Marshal had drunk at the bar in the past fortnight. Instead, he asked after Grace - and if her bookshop was still flourishing.

"Things are going well, thankfully. We even had an author who came in to sign the other day who wasn't conceited... Like you guys, we have some wonderful, loyal customers."

As she spoke the sun came out from behind a clump of clouds. The amber light swept through the window, like a peacock fanning out its tail, and bathed the side of her kind face in lambent gold. The light used to illuminate and soften her features in the morning. First thing on a Sunday they would often read in bed. He remembered reading Flashman and Tolstoy. Grace would read Austen or Flaubert. Somehow, they both knew when to stop reading and make love.

Marshal noticed her hand splayed out on the table. Her bare hand. Her ringless finger both tempted and shamed him. In a different, better, world the light should be shining off a diamond engagement ring or wedding band.

Mike was soon wanted elsewhere, and he left the couple to resume their conversation, or awkward silences.

Marshal finished his coffee, craving a vodka. He remembered how as a raw recruit he would take part in the occasional poker night. He was nicknamed "Bluffer" because he seldom bluffed. The choices in the game resonated with him now. He could "fold" and end the relationship. He told himself that he would be protecting Grace, but there was an element of self-interest, or self-preservation, in the decision too. He could "raise" - go all in - and propose to Grace. Or Marshal could "call" - and allow Grace to determine how the game should play out. The sun retreated behind a dull cloud again. The Phil Collins setlist started, signalling an end to an eighties shuffle. Marshal took a sip of water to wet his dry throat. He felt his voice would break if he spoke - if indeed he could speak at all.

"I only wanted you as someone to love
But something happened on the way to heaven."

He gazed across the table at Grace, hoping to discern some tells. He found himself gripping his knife and fork, as if a meal were about to be served. What was the point of raising - going all in - if he did not know if he would be alive at the end of the day to spend his winnings? If he folded, he might never come back to the table again.

Marry her, or do not marry at all.

Light reflected off the film of sweat forming on his forehead. The cadence of his breathing altered. He felt like he was stuck, sinking, in glutinous mud. Perhaps it might be best if the world just swallowed him up. He was tempted to excuse himself and pretend he needed the toilet. For a moment, Marshal felt like breaking into a smile, or laughter. He had been in better possession of himself when he had gunned down Viktor Baruti and tortured and executed Nolan. His chest throbbed, as if his heart might turn into a Catherine wheel, which was just about to break free from the nail holding it in place. *Raise or fold. Raise or fold. Raise or fold.* There was another option, however, one that he regularly employed during smoke and booze filled nights playing poker, all those years ago. The sun came out from behind the clouds once more. Or seemed to. He could, would, "check" - and defer making any decision.

"I know that I do not deserve it, Grace, but I would ask that you have faith in me for a little while longer," Marshal said - pleaded.

I might then have a little more faith in me.

"This too shall pass," he added. "I just feel like a man who is still trying to dig his way out of a hole. But have faith in me. Have faith that I'm sorry. Forgive me, as it will help me forgive myself. God knows that I can be a wretch sometimes, a pilgrim who has barely made any progress."

Grace had never known a man to talk like Marshal. Or be like Marshal. He was from a different, better, age. The Catholic would forgive the penitent. She loved him, more than he knew.

Marshal had ticked the box to say sorry. But he felt too drained, or cowardly, to say goodbye. Grace would be too confused, ask too many questions, if he said goodbye. He willed his hand not to tremble as he took another sip of water. Oliver would explain certain things to Grace, should his mission fail, he judged. There would be more questions than answers, but that was only to be expected. Marshal hoped that grief would not put her in a hole that she could not dig her way out of. On more than one occasion, over the past day, he had imagined Grace standing beside his grave, crying. She looked good in black, of course.

Oliver Porter sat in his study at the top of the house. Violet lay content on the deep pile patterned carpet, keeping one eye open, in the hope that her master might open the treat drawer in his rosewood desk. A framed print of Goya's portrait of the Duke of Wellington hung on the wall above the desk. The Iron Duke. Porter removed a *Romeo y Julieta* from its case and ran the length of the cigar under his nose. An ornate, polished bronze and silver cigar cutter and a sleek, chrome cigar lighter sat beside his laptop. Porter never tired of the small ritual of lighting and smoking a cigar. He loved it, even more than his wife disapproved of the habit. Porter felt he had earned his reward. He had written a thousand words, or a thousand good enough words, of his historical novel during the morning. He thought that he might finish a first draft by the end of November. He imagined that he would feel a sense of satisfaction and trepidation once he finished. He would tentatively send the manuscript out to literary agents. He wondered what he could do to help fix himself a book deal. He would be willing to threaten or bribe an agent perhaps, but not become a celebrity or employ a ghost writer.

Porter was about to cut the end of the cigar, savouring the moment, when his phone rang. The caller ID was an unknown number, but Marshal had warned him that he may call on a burner.

"Hello," Porter said, offering up a tone of six out of ten on his cordiality meter.

"Today will be the day," Marshal remarked, without ceremony. His voice was a harlequin pattern of confidence and diffidence. To have sounded any different would have been unnatural, Porter mused.

"It doesn't have to be, should you be having any doubts. You can still walk away, James. No one would know," Porter said, in hope more than expectation.

"I would know."

"It's a gamble."

"One worth taking."

Porter worried that his friend may have been descending into zealotry. He was a strange fish, the fixer thought. Marshal looked equally at ease carrying a copy of Kierkegaard as he did carrying a gun. He remembered when he first met the PMC, looking for work.

"You may have to work for some unpleasant people," Porter warned.

"I just like to call them people," Marshal replied, darkly or jokingly.

Porter had characterised Marshal as being indifferent, all those years ago. He seemed more zealous than indifferent now, to his detriment.

Smoking the cigar did not seem as appealing now, as he stared at the *Romeo y Julieta* before him. Churchill had smoked the same brand. Porter took a deep breath, as if he were about to say something of import, but he merely emitted a sigh, as opposed to any sage words.

"I just want to assure you, Oliver, that I have taken steps so that, if I am apprehended or worse, Mullen or the authorities will not be able to trace anything untoward back to you," Marshal said, intending to dump the burner phone he was using on the way to the offices in Mornington Crescent. "I also have one last favour to ask. Should something go awry this afternoon, can you put the video in the right hands? It may be summer, but Martin Coulson would welcome it as an early Christmas present."

Porter sighed, or huffed, a little. More than he intended to do. Perhaps he was disapproving that Marshal was going ahead with things, or that the avenging angel was dragging him back to his former life. The fixer had retired. Retirement had been good for the soul. Unlike Marshal, Porter did not feel an itch, in his trigger finger or elsewhere, to fix things. Fixing something for one person usually meant breaking something else for someone else. Porter promised that he would pass the evidence on, though. Marshal would have the last laugh, even when he was dead. His revenge would outlive him.

"I must ask a favour of you in return," Porter asserted. "But I will tell you another time. You will need to be still with us, of course, to carry out any favour."

Marshal failed to mention his recent meeting with Grace during their conversation. He told himself that there was insufficient time to discuss the matter. But, in truth, Marshal did not want to be reminded of his callous behaviour. He knew how much he had sinned. He did not need Porter to point it out too.

After he ended the call, Marshal changed into jeans, a nondescript (reversible) jacket and baseball cap. He was more than willing to appear anonymous looking at any time, but today, especially, he wanted to be forgettable. He closed his eyes and visualised the list that Mariner had sent him, where certain surveillance cameras were in place - and how to avoid them. The cap would duly shield his face too. The black sports bag was already packed, containing a Glock 21 - replete with suppressor - along with a few other items. There was already a round in the chamber. If all went well with the plan, he would only need one round.

Man plans, God laughs.

20.

Marshal walked with an uncommon purpose. He was almost marching, like he was a soldier again. A black cab had dropped him off, half a mile from the offices in North London. *Death and taxies.* He had flagged the cab down, half a mile from his home. As much as Marshal was determined to murder Mullen, he was also infected by a bout of fatalism. It cast a pall over his thoughts, like a veil falling over a widow's face. He judged that he could well be heading towards his own demise - but he didn't much care. It didn't much matter. Marshal remembered how, before taking part in patrols in various hotspots in Helmand, he would recite a passage from Shakespeare in his mind. He did so again now.

"Be absolute for death; for either death or life
Shall thereby be the sweeter. Reason thus with life, -
If I do lose thee, I do lose a thing
That none but fools would keep."

Rather than descending into a debilitating bleakness, Marshal felt emancipated, edified. He felt a little light-headed, giddy, like an epileptic feels before a fit. The tweeters, Lycra-clad cyclists and Liberal Democrats failed to bother him, as he walked past them. They did not matter either. They would scatter in the wind, like everything else. Nothing mattered, except ending Mullen. The future would then take care of itself. If he died, he died. Everything is born to die. Marshal mused that he had been on the planet - a world which he was far from enamoured with - for long enough. Or too long. The dull ache in his stomach, which had gnawed away at him for as long as he could remember, subsided.

Marshal could tell himself that Grace mattered. But it would be a lie, albeit a beautiful one. Like the idea of faith and God. But maybe they were lies worth telling. Otherwise, he would have been even less enamoured with the world. If only there was an English word for "ennui" he jokingly thought. Marshal realised that he needed to laugh more - at himself and others. Laughter, along with whisky, was the best medicine.

Disparate clouds clumped together, reforming like a sea sponge. The marbled sky reminded Marshal of the colour of his grandfather's gravestone. He chided himself for not visiting the cemetery more often. It was another venial sin, to add to the list. His grandfather would have approved of his decision to avenge Foster's death. For him, there may not have even been a choice to make. *Who dares, wins*. Marshal was certainly being daring. Whether he would win or not was a different matter.

There was still time to fold. But the gambler would raise - go all in. Marshal was around ten minutes away from his end point. Or endgame. He would walk through some backstreets. The route was longer, but the CCTV cameras were fewer. He went over a few things in his mind again, recalling the various escape routes. He rehearsed his lines if, somehow, he was apprehended by the police. He remembered the smoke grenades in his bag, to be used should he need a distraction to cover his retreat. He recalled the locations where he could potentially drop the bag. He had handled the contents whilst wearing latex gloves and made sure that no hair follicles had accidentally fallen into the bag. His inner eye pored over the images of Duggan's security personnel, as if viewing a book of mugshots. Watchers could be lining his route. The question, which might soon be answered, was would they recognise him?

People yammered into their phones, or hypnotically stared at the screens. Couriers and takeaway delivery drivers still zipped by him. Cars clogged up the arteries of the road. London still throbbed and thrummed, but there were few tourists or schoolchildren in the area. The streets were relatively quiet. The exodus of office workers was still an hour or so away.

His forehead itched, but Marshal resisted the temptation to remove his cap. His palms perspired. His heart pounded, in harmony with his footsteps on the dark grey pavement. The skies grew more funereal. Sepulchral. He felt naked, exposed, without his gun in his hand. Helmand could be considered safer, compared to the potential kill zone he was advancing into. *Into the valley of death.* Marshal could not quite decide if he was quoting Tennyson or scripture. He could not quite decide if he should picture Grace, his grandfather, Foster or Mullen before he turned into the relevant street – like a condemned man trying to decide on his last meal.

At least it will soon be over, one way or another.

The breeze swirled a little, but would not factor into the shot, Sean Duggan judged. The round had been chambered. He rubbed his stubbled cheek against the sniper rifle, like a cat affectionately rubbing against its master, and flexed the hand containing his trigger finger. The weapon had never misfired, jammed or let him down. People let you down. Never a well-maintained rifle. The stock of the sniper rifle, replete with suppressor, was nestled in his shoulder. The violent zealot licked his lips. His heart pounded in anticipation of the shot. The kill. The adrenaline rush rivalled any bout of lust or a drug high. He checked his watch, again.

Soon.

"Just don't fucking miss," Mullen had ordered that morning, wagging a finger in the air.

"I didn't miss with Byrne. I won't miss this bastard either. He's so fucking full of himself, he's got such a big head, that the target will loom large," Duggan replied, whilst carefully cleaning the rifle's sight.

Mullen nodded and smiled a little, recalling the death of Byrne. Duggan had called him after the shot. Mullen immediately looked out of his office window and down at the corpse. Blood, brain, flesh and bone decorated the pavement, as Duggan's bullet had torn half his head off. Blood began to ooze out of the well-attired cadaver too, like oil leaking from a sump. Passers-by understandably fled, whilst screaming. He remembered one witness shout, "God, no!" *God, yes,* Mullen had thought in return, eminently satisfied. An opponent had been removed from the game. It had been a good day. Hopefully, today would be too, the Irishman mused.

The enforcer wore a grey tracksuit, to blend in with the colour of the roof on the opposite building to their office block. The ledge on the roof was wide and he could lay down. The roof was also slightly higher than surrounding structures. The vantage point looked down slightly on his building. He would be firing down on his target at a pronounced, but far from impossible angle. A pair of *Canon All Weather* binoculars sat next to the sniper. He could just about make out who was coming and going from the foyer of the building with the naked eye, but he would use the binoculars to spot any prospective target approaching. His phone also lay in reach too. Mullen had instructed the sniper to call him as soon as he had taken the shot. Or not. Similarly, his man inside the foyer had been briefed to call Duggan should someone approach the reception and collect the briefcase. The blackmailer could well have a team of associates. More than one target could enter the foyer too. Duggan knew from first-hand experience that criminals should not altogether be trusted.

The sniper increasingly believed that he was dealing with a lone wolf, though. He had pored over various intelligence files the evening before. He was doubtful that his target could be a rogue paramilitary - Catholic or Protestant - who had a grievance against his paymaster, but he nevertheless did his due diligence. Duggan also examined photographs of John Foster's associates in the army, who were willing and able to act against them – including the ex-Paratrooper he drank with on the day of his abduction. His nephew had taken a picture of the Brit on his phone. If the former soldier somehow proved to be their lone wolf, the hunter would soon become prey.

A few silhouettes flitted past the frosted glass, but Mullen had given strict instructions for no one to enter and disturb him. His staff would be worried about their jobs. They should be, he thought.

There was a scenario where the blackmailer successfully took the money, avoided Duggan's crosshairs and disappeared, never to be heard of again, as he promised. There was also a scenario where the blackmailer's courier was taken out by his sniper. The violent act might give the blackmailer pause. He needed to realise that he was dealing with a big beast in the jungle. Mullen had already instructed his Head of Security to reach out to certain contacts, to obtain intelligence on their enemy. Once they had a name, they could look to secure justice. It had taken over three decades for Mullen to carry out his revenge against the guilty party who had murdered his son. Hopefully, vengeance would come sooner, in relation to his current opponent.

Mullen swivelled back and forth in his chair with metronomic regularity. He tapped his finger on his mouse, as if he were sending a telegram in the Old West.

Duggan was in position.

Soon.

His screen flashed, alerting the politician to a new email. It had been forwarded on by Caitlin. He did not care now whether she wore a trouser suit or not. The message informed him of another cancellation for a speaking engagement. He had been booked in to speak to a congregation in Dublin. Even the Catholic Church now judged him as being toxic.

A few blue pills, in a tiny plastic packet, sat on the desk. They prompted Mullen to click on another window on the screen, displaying an array of high-end escorts. It was time to shop for a new mistress, for tonight or longer. He needed a distraction, release, from various problems. The girl would need to be discrete. Under forty. His preference was for someone Irish, or at least not British. His mouth hung open as he devoured the glamorous images. Drool might well have run down his chin at any moment. Mullen felt a slight pang when he scrolled down and noticed "Satin", a Polish escort who resembled Josephine. He was tempted to call his former lover once more. If he could just talk to Josephine, even for five minutes. The statesman believed he was sufficiently charming or intimidating to cause a change of heart in the woman. He missed her. He would even be willing to offer his mistress more money to be with him.

A burner phone lay next to the Viagra. Duggan could call at any moment. Mullen had watched the video of Foster's torture and execution again, the previous evening. As compromising as the video was, it might not be completely damning. The former terrorist could, just about, claim plausible deniability. Nolan had not mentioned his involvement during the gruesome clip. His alibi would still count for something. Nolan was, most likely, dead. Without a witness for the prosecution to link the statesman to the murder, the case would flounder. It was a gamble - to take out the blackmailer at the risk of the video being released - but one worth taking. Again, the authorities would consider him the prime suspect, but there would be no concrete evidence to charge him for the man's murder. His reputation would be in tatters, but Mullen currently had little to lose on that front. With his political career over, he reasoned that he would be freer to return to certain criminal and terrorist activities. His ruin could be the making of him. If his wife met with an accident, Mullen would have the funds to rebuild too, sooner rather than later.

Marshal wiped his palm on his trousers, in anticipation of pulling out his gun. Ready for anything. Even now, it was not too late to turn back. Although he did not regret writing any suicide note - before looking to complete his suicide mission - Marshal did feel a wave of remorse in not writing a letter to Grace. But what's done is done. Marshal quickened his pace even more. He refused to walk with leaden footsteps, like a condemned man approaching the gallows. His heart thumped, as if each beat were powerful enough to hammer a nail into a coffin. Porter had, at one point, called him "mad", after pursuing his course of action and revealing his plan. Marshal replied, with a half-smile:

"I am but mad north-north-west."

Nothing is good or bad but thinking makes it so.

His heart felt as black and hard as the asphalt beneath his feet.

Mullen wiped his sweaty palm, before picking up the phone and answering it.

"I got the bastard. I recognised him. He served with Foster. I took him out before he could even get to the offices. Do yourself a favour and look out the window, to your right. I have to go now," the sniper said, a little breathlessly, before his boss could even offer him a word of thanks. Mullen could forgive his lieutenant for wanting to quickly abscond and leave the building opposite through the rear entrance.

Mullen puffed out his cheeks and thanked God - or congratulated himself on the success of his bold plan. The "Big

Man" could still be judged as such. The Irishman looked like a happy Brendan Gleeson, his face flush with joy and booze. Mullen wondered whether there would be a crowd forming around the body, or if people would be fleeing. No doubt the police would question him, in relation to the assassination, but the politician would bat any questions away like flies. A wave of relief and triumph ran through him. It felt something akin to a religious experience. A Holy Spirit.

He took a sip of *Bushmills*, slapped the desk, and got to his feet. Mullen flipped the catches on the large windows, weighed down by the thick glass. The sun was coming out. The grey clouds were dissipating, like butter melting in a pan. It was going to be a glorious afternoon.

21.

Mullen lifted the window up, thrust his head out and looked to the right. For a moment he felt confused. And then he felt nothing. The bullet smashed through the bridge of his nose and exploded through the back of his skull, as if he were being punched squarely in the face by a god.

Marshal didn't hesitate and he didn't miss. He had gambled on Duggan being posted on the building opposite, similar to the hit on Tom Byrne. The gamble paid off. He was dressed in a balaclava when he surprised Duggan on the roof, whose focus was on the street below. Marshal wore latex gloves, as he gripped the Glock.

Duggan spat out a curse in Gaelic. Marshal didn't know what he was saying, he just sensed that it wasn't particularly flattering. The enforcer complied, when Marshal instructed him to remove the weapon, replete with suppressor, from his shoulder holster and toss it towards him. Up close, Marshal fancied that Duggan resembled a ginger, humourless Desperate Dan. He noticed a tattoo of a Celtic cross on his neck. The ink was the same colour as the burst blood vessels on his nose and cheeks. Duggan was torn between two thoughts/expressions. He looked like he wanted to kill the man in front of him - but not be killed by him too. He was more defeated than defiant though. Even cocaine would have failed to lift his mood. If the shooter had not fired already, though, there was a chance he could still live.

"I am not here for you, I'm here for Mullen. He was the one who ultimately pulled the trigger on Foster," Marshal said, his voice as hard as titanium. "If I was intending to kill you, I would not be wearing a balaclava." It was another beautiful lie, which

Duggan saw the logic of. Perhaps because he wanted to believe it so much. "Follow my instructions and you will get to walk away from this. But I will pull the trigger on you, if you fail to comply - or if you bore me."

If Duggan got the blackmailer's joke at the end, it did not prompt him laugh. The enforcer squinted in the sunlight and glanced up at his enemy. *The Brit bastard.* Duggan looked into his eyes and recognised a fellow killer. He wasn't bluffing. Even the most ardent zealot will be gripped by pragmatism and rationality when someone is holding a gun to their head. Self-preservation would be sovereign over his loyalty to his friend. The two men had been through a lot together over the years, but that did not mean that they had to die together.

"Why the fuck are you doing this?" Duggan asked, his voice rough with resentment - as if he were gargling bile.

"I wanted bad things to happen to bad people. Now call your boss and read out what's on this piece of paper," Marshal replied, whilst retrieving the note from his pocket and handing it to Duggan.

The Head of Security made the call. Simmering and cowed at the same time. His eyes flitted back and forth between the paper and the Glock, hovering a yard away from his face.

"I got the bastard. I recognised him…"

As soon as Duggan ended the call, Marshal picked up his opponent's weapon and, without a word being said, spat out a round into the enforcer's temple from just a few inches away. Death preserved the look of astoundment on his expression. The was a flicker of emotion from the shooter, for the duration of the report of the gun, but then it was over. Foster would have nodded his head in approval, his friend imagined. Marshal felt like he was finally atoning for his sins. He did not even the need the round chambered in his own gun. Using Duggan's pistol would add more weight to the narrative of a murder suicide, he reasoned.

Marshal quickly lay down, checked the rifle was ready to fire, and moved the crosshairs into position. The butt of the weapon slotted into his shoulder, like a dovetail joint. The window opened. Mullen's head appeared, as bulbous as a melon, through the sight. The shooter could even make out the liver spots on his forehead. Marshal took a breath, squeezed the trigger, and breathed out. The sudden recoil took him back to Helmand. But only for a second.

Caitlin heard a strange, disturbing sound come from Mullen's office. The secretary had been given strict orders not to disturb her boss, however, and was unable to see anything through the frosted glass.

Marshal descended the deserted stairway briskly, removing the balaclava and latex gloves. He reversed his jacket and donned a different baseball cap, which he retrieved from his bag. The sun had come out. It was going to be a glorious afternoon.

22. Epilogue.

Marshal was tempted to pack a bag and leave the country for a month, the day after the killings. He was confident that his plan had worked, but he still understandably imagined that he could receive a knock on the door at any moment. Man plans, God laughs. He reasoned, though, that he might draw suspicion to himself by leaving the country, where an absence of suspicion currently existed.

Thankfully, there was no knock at the door. And if guilt or grief still knocked on his door at night, then they did so less vigorously. Marshal was content. He had kept his word. Kept his honour.

The news reported that Sean Duggan, for reasons yet unknown, had assassinated his employer, John Mullen. He then turned his gun on himself. The violent killings were billed as the news story of the year, for a week.

Marshal was determined to carry on as normal. He had a drink and watched some football at *The Tap-In* with Paul. The following evening, he had a curry with Chef, Mike and Yohann. They even played some poker. Marshal didn't bluff - and he didn't win. Things were returning to normal. Was his "normal" life one with or without Grace, however?

When questioned about events, Mary Mullen, clasping a set of rosary beads, diplomatically commented that her husband was now in a better place. Privately, the churchgoer was unsure whether even God could forgive the depraved murderer and adulterer for his sins. Mary called her accountant first upon hearing the tragic news, and then she called the local funeral directors to make the requisite arrangements. She chose the cheapest casket. She was also mindful of keeping the service small and not allowing the television cameras in, because her husband would have wanted the opposite.

Teresa Mullen took centre stage for the media after her father's dramatic murder. She was angry (although some of the anger was confected) and demanded justice. "My father had his faults, but he did not deserve to die... He was a fine Irishman, who believed in peace and a united Ireland." She wanted to find out the truth, if her father's death was linked to a conspiracy or cover-up. She hinted that her father was a victim of "the British establishment", but could not be any clearer, or vaguer, when questioned about her assertions. Teresa Mullen was willing to do anything to get justice for her father, including charging a fee for every interview and press conference she took part in. Allan Boyle first offered his sympathies, on behalf of Sinn Fein, before offering Teresa Mullen the opportunity to run for her father's seat in the forthcoming by-election. She looked good on camera and a number of focus-groups responded positively to her "authenticity". "She is like the Irish Liz Truss or Esther McVey," one focus group member argued. Although "Mullen" was not altogether a name the public could trust, it did have name recognition, which carried nearly equal currency for the party hierarchy (albeit some of the female members of the Sinn Fein seemed less keen on the telegenic woman's candidacy).

Josephine Quinn made herself unavailable for comment. Her father, on more than one occasion, had to chase off a few bottom-feeding, door-stepping journalists from the front of his property. Josephine wanted to put the past behind her. In return for her mother agreeing to put a roof over her head, Josephine promised to re-start her nursing training. At the same time, she also contacted her old web designer, to ask him to create a new site for her. Her past would also be her future. Josephine dyed her hair blonde and arranged for some new pictures to be taken. "Beauty" would re-launch herself as "Mystique".

"The world is a slightly finer place with Mullen and Duggan absent from it," Martin Coulson's commanding officer argued. "Sign-off on the investigation. Take the win."

Coulson agreed, reluctantly. There were a couple of moments when he had a mind to investigate James Marshal and tug upon any thread that might come loose. Not everything added up, in relation to motive and the crime scene. There were more questions than answers. But that was life.

The policeman signed-off on the case. He was owed some leave, and had promised Irene that he would catch-up on some work in the garden. He had also just found out that his daughter had joined *Extinction Rebellion*.

God help us.

Porter made some subtle inquiries into the shootings, the day after. He also tasked Mariner to keep him abreast of any developments. At no point was Marshal a person of interest. Porter blew a sigh of relief, both for his friend and for himself. There did not seem to be any danger of things coming back to him.

Life could carry on as normal. Porter continued to fly-fish, work on his novel and eat more foie gras than his wife, doctor or any vegan would approve of. He also often walked in on his wife when she was having a heart to heart with her niece over the phone. Instead of keeping an ear out for any gossip, Porter was mindful of just walking out of the room again, without being seen. He did not want to get overly involved in fixing Marshal's faltering relationship.

I'm retired.

But not altogether retired. Porter still had to call in his favour from his friend. Marshal duly agreed to take care of Violet whilst Porter and his wife went away on holiday. The sweet-natured mongrel could not stop wagging her tail in a windmill motion when she settled into Marshal's flat. Similarly, Marshal could not stop smiling when the dog clambered over him and licked his face with uncommon affection. The ex-soldier could never be unhappy in the company of the dog.

The following day Marshal was sitting outside of Bobo in the massaging sunshine, with Violet at his feet, keeping one eye open for one of the staff coming out with an obligatory dog treat. He had just finished writing an email to Billy Turney, discussing the prospect of investing in his courier business. His phone vibrated with a message from Grace:

Hi. I hope you're well. Oliver said that you are looking after Violet for the next fortnight. Let me know if you would like some help walking her.

Marshal put down his drink and replied:

I would love that. So would Violet. Call me when free. Xx.

Within a few seconds of sending the text, his Blackberry chimed. He felt he should no longer leave his screensaver blank.

Raise, don't fold, Marshal thought to himself as he answered the call.

Printed in Great Britain
by Amazon